SLIVER OF TRUTH

JODY KAYE

Special Edition Paperback

First Print: January 2024

www.JodyKaye.com

____

Splinter of Hope
Shred of Decency
Sliver of Truth
Holding Onto Hope
Home Wrecker
Deep Gap
Bleeding Heart
Shattered Soul

*I hate that I love
the strength of his arms.
I love that I hate it, too.
The feeling keeps me sane.*

Your greatest contribution may not be something you do, but someone you raise.

Chapter One

Celine

Water swirls down the drain of the old clawfoot tub as I wrap myself in a fluffy white bath sheet. I take the smaller one I've twisted around my head off, rubbing my scalp to wick as much of the moisture away so I'm not stuck blow drying my hair. The ends split on my long brown locks when I do. Year-round, the North Carolina heat does mighty fine on its own without my meddling. However, we're enduring a mid-December cold snap and wet hair makes me chilly. I'd used the hot bath to warm my bones and limber my muscles before work.

Other dancers at Sweet Caroline's swear by wigs. For me, they're a job hazard. I apply enough tape to keep my costume in place and prefer not stabbing my scalp with bobby pins. I've been stripping long enough to have watched hairpieces go flying across the stage, landing in a patron's lap like the pelt of a dead rodent.

A giggle escapes me, bouncing off the vaulted ceiling. Everyone should have memories that make them laugh.

I'm so darn relaxed it's easy to forget I'm about to

spend the next few hours as the evening's headline showgirl parading around in sky-high fuck-me pumps and wearing less than my bathing suit covers. This is my last night on stage. Within the week, I'm graduating from the physician's assistant program and will finally finish school. The past few days have been the most time I've had to myself in forever. Thank goodness clinicals are done and over with, and don't even get me started on how hard the prior year was. They ground us into the dirt, weeding out survivors with each exam. This month, I scored a nine-to-five in Dr. Randolph's clinic, a pediatrician who I'd shadowed. After tonight, dancing is my past and I have a whole new future.

The steam in the tiny washroom is like a sauna, and the linens I pulled from the shelf are the sort you'd expect at an expensive day spa. Thank heaven the ladies who live on the third floor at the mill have what we need, even if we hadn't known we needed anything this decadent.

None of us are footsteps away from slumming it at the no-tell motel anymore. Each of us has a story, most of which is made up of the nastier stuff in fairytales; those low points of abandonment and loss swept under the carpet because what folks remember about bedtime stories are the parts where everyone lives happily ever after. For girls who grew up the way we did, getting to the point where, on our own, we didn't have to figure out where the next meal was coming from was half the battle. I'm fortunate I've never had to choose between selling my soul or affording my rent and tuition. But I came damn close to choosing if they were worth going hungry for before Jake hired me at Sweet Caroline's. A few months later, he set me up with Carver, the mill's owner.

Living at the old cotton factory is an enviable spot to be in. Carver foots the bill for our living expenses while each of us attends college. Although given all that goes unsaid around this place, I figure it's pragmatic to understand Carver has a vested interest in what we become. I've yet to figure out his endgame for me. Nobody's that altruistic.

I run my razor over a spot I missed near my ankle while soaking. I'm between waxes and I swear those little patches sneak up when you're positive your skin is pristine. I understand the audience is none the wiser when I'm on stage—and it's not as if they'll lie down on the stale carpeting to inspect my Achilles Heel—but it matters to me. Maybe because the last time I saw my mother she had a whisker on her chin and a glower on her face.

Is it pathetic, while I was quick to get over feeling like a slut taking off my clothes on stage in front of all of those men, that I still worry over every nasty remark my mother would make if she knew I afforded my tuition by dancing? Defending my actions against her judgmental words are the ugly phrases on repeat in my head while getting to this point. Mom's transgressions never seem to bother her. Soon enough it won't make a difference. I'm proud of myself for achieving my dreams instead of succumbing to her nightmare.

Rubbing lemon and basil scented lotion over my arms, my mind wanders back to happier thoughts. Against the odds, my brother, Morgan, and I have stuck together like glue. He wasn't thrilled at my choice to become a stripper, though he picked up shifts at the club to monitor my safety which means everything to him. That right there reminds me I have someone to count on. My best friends—who started out up here as my floormates—are also with men willing to walk over broken glass for them. With the changes about to happen in my life, the last thing I have the energy for is a relationship. But a girl can hope the notion of the right guy coming along when you least expect it rings true.

I can't help the dismissive shrug of my shoulders. What's meant to be has a way of working out. One thing I've realized is luck's more likely to shine on those who are prepared, and I have a plan for the next few years.

A thump on the other side of the wall has me cracking open the door to the little room where the original to the factory building antique clawfoot is. I glance around the bigger bathroom area with its clean bright tiles and periwinkle blue, sage green, and light tan shabby chic beach house decor. A tap drips along the far wall where multiple sinks are set into an immense marble countertop. Gooseflesh appears on my skin while I wonder for a second if I hadn't turned the handle all the way off. Not seeing anything else out of the ordinary, I leave the frosted glass door ajar, stepping out to put my stuff away in the decorative locker-style cubbies. I appreciate not having to lug shampoo and bath bombs down the hall in a caddy.

When I started college, I'd have jumped in with both feet given the chance to live in Pinewood's dorms. They'd seemed like the epitome, a normal experience out of my grasp. Now, I'm glad I lost out on the opportunity. My friendships at the mill have meant so much more.

As I place my razor, lotion, and a bottle of bubbles on the shelf, a calloused knuckle grazes my bare upper arm.

"Cees."

His voice is a guttural growl I feel at the apex of my thighs.

My pulse speeds up and my breaths grow shallow. I want nothing more than to tell Dusty "No". This has gone on long enough. I should have stopped it before it started, but resisting proved futile.

His fingertips skim the hem of the towel, pushing the soft cotton up over my ass. He cups each globe. The rough fabric of his jeans scratches against my bare skin as he moves closer, caging me in. Dusty's lips touch my neck, sending anxious chills down to my toes. "Door's locked. Nobody's around."

I swallow hard and try to look over my shoulder.

The standing rule is women only on this floor. Not all of the rooms are occupied anymore, but the ladies who live here have always worked at Sweet Caroline's. I'm sure Carver's edict is to stop us from bringing clients home. He's forthright, refusing to accept any of us turning tricks on his property. What we do at Sweet Caroline's and outside these four walls is our own nevermind. But Carver's insistent the rule also serves a greater purpose: to keep us safe. Mindful of what kind of people are out there, it's difficult to argue with.

No man other than Dusty goes past the last step before the landing. He's allowed a free pass because he's the maintenance guy here and over at the club. Everyone trusts him. I trusted him more than I had myself, and should have said no to his advances on the night he took Morgan's place and walked me home. Ever since, I've lost count of the number of instances Dusty's left me with his cum dripping down my thighs.

The first dozen times I was sure we'd be found out. Then, recognizing I broke Carver's cardinal rule, shame made me more concerned with keeping this secret closely guarded.

"Don't make a sound," Dusty warns me the way he always does.

I bite my lip, hearing the metallic zip of his fly coming undone. He thrusts his impossibly huge cock inside of me, and I whimper.

I hate that I love this. I love that I hate it too because the feeling keeps me sane.

"Shh... Take it all, Cees. You know you want it."

The warm rush between my legs proves him right. With Dusty, the condemnation of my choices is ever present. I let him do this to me and I don't tell a soul. Admitting we've been fucking for over a year will lead to questions I'm unable to answer.

He removes my palms from the polished lockers, placing them on the cold tiled walls. Dusty drills into me over and over. It's pure ecstasy and I can't stand how wet it gets me. How dirty I feel letting Dusty use me for sexual gratification whenever he damn well pleases, like I'm no more than a toy.

Dusty loosens the knot in my towel. It falls, pinned between his front and my arched back. My nipples are hard points instead of the tender rosy circles they had been when I got out of the water. They ache for attention. His large rough hands knead my breasts, squeezing them as he thrusts, almost as if he's using my tits for leverage to piston himself harder.

As the wave of pleasure builds, I choke down any sounds so they don't reverberate against the tile and walls. I want to scream out. Dusty moves one palm, covering my mouth to keep me quiet. I suck one of his fingers into my mouth, and he murmurs dirty words, urging me closer to the peak of my orgasm. A little mewl hums from me as my tongue swirls the digit and I crest over, my pussy contracting. His climax follows with hot streams of semen painting the inside of me.

I'm stupid for not making him wear a condom, but I've always considered birth control my responsibility and I'm clean. This happens so often I doubt Dusty has the stamina to fuck anyone else. I also lie to myself that even though the sight of this man can stop a woman dead in her tracks, he wouldn't have the opportunity. I'm easy. A sure thing compared to him having to try to get in anyone else's pants. I acknowledge this makes me a bitch. Because if it weren't for me relying on a flimsy excuse, I'd have to admit the gorgeous man inside of me could have any woman he wants.

Dusty's thick arms encircle me, stopping my weak

knees from buckling. My head lolls back against his massive chest and his dark hair and beard brush my cheek. I let out a sigh. He turns my head to shush me, thrusting his tongue into my mouth. We groan together in sorrow. Round two for us is rare.

I know so little about him, and yet I'm cognizant of the safety of his body afterward. The way his lips glide over my skin in reverence. His always-warm palms' lingering touch. We're strangers outside this act, but inside of it? The trust and familiarity are like nothing I've experienced.

He waits before pulling out and when he does it washes the awareness away. He's back to being the lumbering maintenance guy. I'm simply another one of the women who live on the third floor. Dusty doesn't sing praises for my pussy. Ask me if I'm okay. He doesn't need reassurance that I liked it. We're a means to an end for one another. He'll show up again tomorrow or the day after until I'm gone.

I won't confuse what we have as anything more than great sex. And I can't feel sorry if the next occupant of my room winds up pushed against the lockers with her legs spread.

Chapter Two

Dusty

After buckling my belt, I flip the lock, leaving the ladies' room without a goodbye to Celine. Politeness aside, it wouldn't make sense if I did. I'm not supposed to be up here when the girls are around. Someone finding me in the bathroom with her buck naked will draw unwanted attention neither of us is ready to explain.

I pick up some tools I've left in the hall as a deterrent for anyone who might be around when they're not supposed to be and look back at a corkboard hanging on the wall as the door swings shut. The former cotton mill is one of the oldest buildings in Brighton. The girls started posting a schedule when there were big plumbing issues up here. That way I didn't have to ask them to leave when fixing something or worry about interrupting them. They've kept it up since—more for themselves—and it benefits me knowing I can be alone with Cece.

The position I put her in having to lie isn't an easy one. Is it bad after all this time I don't feel worse about chasing her? I should have a hint of remorse she'll need a second soak. But I smirk instead. My spunk is lining her cunt while she's up on stage tonight with customers gawking at her. It's what keeps me focused on Celine throughout her performances instead of jamming my fist through the drywall—that I'm responsible for fixing—pissed at the crowd of men drooling over her.

Opening the enclosed front stairwell door, I hurry down the steps to the living area. I scrub a thick paw over my chin and pause before I reach for the knob. A strand of Cece's brown hair has gotten caught in the scruff of my beard. Glad I caught that. I flip my phone camera to selfie-mode, giving my mug a once over before stuffing it back in the clip and stepping onto the second floor.

Morgan and Skye are sitting on the couches watching some business news channel Skye follows. Technically, they're loafing around. Although I'm sure during the ten minutes I was upstairs screwing Morgan's sister, Skye made us all more money than I earned my last year working as an engineer.

"What did they break this time?" Morgan points at the bucket I carry around with me.

"It was nothing. No installs?" I turn the question of why he's at the factory today back on him.

If Morgan finds out his sister is the one breaking me I'd be a dead man. It was over a year ago my buddy trusted me to walk Cece home from her shift at Sweet Caroline's. He'd had to duck out early and I jumped at the chance to bring her back to the mill safe.

Cece was the only dancer who hadn't interacted with me like I was a lost puppy or a two-year-old. She's compassionate, and that alone is an attractive trait. I didn't feel as if she treated me any different. I never saw pity on her face. She never once talked down to me as if unclogging toilets is all I'm capable of.

My current job isn't rocket science. My last one was,

and it had the same pressure as the flames shooting out of a space shuttle on lift-off. I'd gone back to working for my former employer after the accident. It hadn't lasted long. My cognitive abilities are all there. My speech? I'm more eloquent in my head. No stuttering. No pregnant pauses getting the correct word off of the tip of my tongue. The ability to articulate oneself leaves a lasting impression on people. Unfortunately, the inability to do so once will as well. Back then I'd slip up, get embarrassed. Exhaust myself trying to prove I was still as competent a man as I'd been.

The thing is, the way I look doesn't help matters. Most people never understood my desire to get into a top-notch university when my physique screamed "World Wrestling's Monday Night Headliner". I'd spent years trying to change people's perception. After almost losing my life, I haven't the inclination anymore.

Let people believe what they want to.

Hell, saying I hadn't agreed to take Cece home because of her hot little body is a lie. But I'd hoped she was more than a pretty face before leaning in to kiss her sweet lips. And I was right.

I'm damn proud of her for graduating. The only stupid part is I have no clue how to show or tell her how much. I'm certain testosterone puts me at the disadvantage rather than what anyone implies about my slow speech or aptitude. When it comes to Cece, I really am an idiot.

"Hey, are you even listening?" Morgan breaks my train of thought. I must give him a dumb look because he repeats an abbreviated version of what he's said. "We finished the security upgrade at the medical office Cece's going to work at. Next is installing new cameras for Sweet Caroline's, but Jake's all up in Carver's business, so Trig's been handling that."

"What else is new?" Skye's sarcasm regarding Jake, his older cousin, has us chuckling.

Jake owns Sweet Caroline's. I've got nothing against him. He pays me well to make sure he's not bothered to come in unless it's a genuine emergency. The problem is there is a tendency for urgent issues to arise on the nights he's covering for the club's manager and Jake's the type to leave everyone on edge. The stress is visible on Celine's face then too.

"Glad Cece's done working soon there?" I ask, scrunching my brow while repeating the phrase in my head. I've transposed words because I'm nervous the guys will find out about us at the wrong time. And thinking about Cece always leaves me half hard, which ratchets my anxiety over my friends figuring it out now.

"Hell, yeah." Morgan understands the meaning anyhow. He's confided never being onboard with Cece's choice, but it was hers to make. "I've only stayed on the club's staff because of her. Now that Celine will have a job wearing *actual* clothes, I can be home more nights with Aidy."

"Or you could come out *with* Aidy instead of playing house with Trig and Kimber's kid," Skye's focused on following the ticker at the bottom of the screen.

"I could have sworn you were the one who was up in my business to find a woman a few years back."

"One to fuck the sad sack out of you and get a few jollies with. How was anyone supposed to know you'd wind up with Aidy? I merely proposed getting your dick wet."

Sloan tosses brimming shopping bags over the couch. They land between the other men, startling us all. "I knew."

"You did not." Skye quips, rifling into them and holding up streamers. "What's all this crap?"

"Okay, I didn't." She clutches both of their shoulders. "But what is for sure is that you three are helping decorate this place."

"For Christmas?" I ask. The party supplies Morgan

and Skye pluck from the bags are the wrong color for the holiday, and Sloan hasn't had me haul the ornament boxes up from the basement yet.

Aidy, Hailey, and Kimber tromp up the ancient wooden staircase coming from the reception area where Carver and Trig's businesses are run. The set up below, in the offices on the first floor, is impressive. I won't venture to guess how much of it is legal. Not my circus...

The ladies fling more purchases on top of the guys, laughing. Aidy sits on Morgan's lap, greeting him with a hello kiss. His fingers find the hem of her skirt, tugging it toward her knee.

Hailey settles on the edge of the sofa arm near Skye. She's more animated. "It's for Cece's party after her last show. We're putting it all up before heading over there to watch her."

Skye's pulled his hand away from Hailey's back right before it connects and begins rifling through the bags. "Jasper is letting you go?"

Hailey rolls her eyes, ignoring the intrusive question as she snatches a metallic congratulations banner out of Skye's grasp.

I'm not sure how much Celine knows about her own party, though Sloan extended an open invitation to drop in to everyone at the mill and Cece's coworkers at the club.

"If it's a surrprise, hide it. She's still around." The blood hasn't made its way back up to my brain again, and I've opened my mouth too soon by mistake. Plus, my rush to warn them has me tripping up, double pronouncing my Rs. It's something I focus damn hard on and heat pools at my collar.

Morgan pegs me with a scowl.

"She was there." I stick a finger in the direction of the steps to the third floor. "When I'd gone to check the ladies' room."

"Thanks for telling us, Dusty." Sloan's grateful. I've lost track of the surprise parties she's planned.

Everyone's almost got the balloons and packages of confetti put away when we hear footsteps coming from the landing near the wall of windows.

"What are you all up to?" Celine arches a brow, spying the seven of us sitting on the couches trying to act nonchalant.

Like usual, Cece's waiting until she gets across the street to do her makeup. Her hair is curling, but she'll straighten and style it before going on stage. She has on a gray sweatsuit to stay warm with "secret" splashed up the side in burgundy block lettering. The word mocks me. She's twirling an umbrella in one hand.

"They're biding time before your last performance. We, however, don't want to be late when Jake's got your image splashed on the marquee." Kimber loops her arm into Cece's. She's the club's manager. "It'll be a packed house tonight."

Celine hikes her duffle on her shoulder, glancing at the bags Aidy and Hailey have tried to hide under the coffee table. "I told you not to go out of your way."

"Do you think your last dance and graduation are the only reasons to throw a party?" Sloan teases.

"No, but it's one you'll use. I said, 'no fuss' when you talked me into a few people afterward. Swear to me, it's only you guys."

Sloan bends her arm, giving Celine a wonky version of a scout promise.

Cece doesn't seem convinced. The fingers of her empty hand splay into a diminutive wave directed at her brother. "I'll see you later."

I'm not happy I'm invisible, but she hasn't paid much attention to Skye either. I ignore the ache in my chest and the overwhelming desire to pull Cece onto my lap the way Morgan had when Aidy entered the room. Kiss Cees. Tell her to break a leg. Be the one to bring her home to the party instead of her brother doing it. Reassure her she deserves the effort her girls are putting into making tonight special.

I listen, tuned into the soft scuffing of her ballerina flats as Kimber and Cece descend the stairs. We wait until we hear the heavy front door close before Sloan gives each of us a task.

Skye flips the television to a Christmas music station. "We're on to you, Sloan," he grumbles. "As soon as this party is over, you'll make Morgan and I move the pool tables to put up the tree."

"Oh, poor things." She squeezes my bicep and then pats where she touched, giving me a friendly wink. "Where on earth will you and Morgan find a big strong man to help you weaklings?"

My chest rumbles. Sloan's all right. I like how she's making Cece's celebration a priority before the big bash Carver throws on Christmas Eve.

"For implying Dusty is stronger, we're not listening to Bing Crosby." Skye changes the channel to a nineties grunge and modern alternative playlist.

Aidy takes me in from head to toe. "I'm sorry, Morgan, but Dusty could lift the flipping couch single-handed." She snorts.

"With all of us on top of it." Hailey agrees.

I take the girls' compliments for what they are, but Morgan shoots me another glower I don't want to read into.

Chapter Three

Sloan, Aidy, and Hailey do a fantastic job of decking out the room in Pinewood College school colors and spangled sparkly banners. For as much as Skye bitched, we've sat around waiting on them to tell us what to do and then jumping to it out of boredom. The girls leave the cleanup to us and dart off to change before we all head over to the club to see Cece's show. Anyone with a dick is wearing what they've got on; jeans and a t-shirt.

Trying to ignore the evil eye Morgan won't stop shooting in my direction, I've spent most of my time sending a string of unnecessary texts, checking in to remind Renata I won't need supper. I live about five miles away with my ex-fiancee's mother. Renata wouldn't consider my offer to stop squatting at her house after Beth died. Most evenings I go home for dinner and come back if there's an emergency. Renata understands sometimes my schedule can be unpredictable, and she leaves me a plate if I haven't called to say I'm running late.

I'm excited for Cece, but fold up the ladders feeling

less than involved. I'd like to do something nice for her the way I have for the other women in my life.

I wrap a burly paw around the metal, stopping to drop the ladder to let Carver up the main staircase. He slaps me on the shoulder with his usual air of confidence. I grunt in acknowledgment as he disappears into the two-bedroom suite off the main living area where he lives with Sloan.

Ruminating on how unfair his situation is in comparison, it dawns on me Sloan had a room on the third floor before they'd gotten involved with one another. Rocket scientist or not, I've drilled it into my head for as long as Cece lives at the mill, she's off-limits. I've also used the excuse that hiding what we're doing legitimizes its wrongness.

Every question about my competence rushes at me full force. I'm a dolt. For over a year, I've had the chance to sit Celine on my lap. Hold her hand in public and kiss her. I could have asked her out and put a stop to our sneaking around.

Outing our transgression, rocking the boat, hadn't only seemed like the last option, it didn't seem like a choice at all. Deep in my subconscious, I've hoped Cece would ask if we could hang out when neither of us were busy. When she hadn't brought it up, I gave her space. Perhaps what she's looking for in a relationship is nothing more than explosive chemistry, and we've got that.

I scrub my face. Fuck, I was more concerned with being close to her, letting her use me, then admit if she turned me down our escapade would cease. I didn't want to admit she didn't like me as much as she liked what I was doing to her.

Now, I can't shake the feeling that I've been giving Cece the same impression. I'm ashamed of myself for not putting her needs first and making her think all I've ever been interested in is sex.

Our primary mode of communication is moans and filthy requests. I should have been talking to her all this time. I've likely given her the impression I can't string a sentence together that doesn't include more than the same three words; suck, my, and dick.

I want to make it up to her, and there isn't a better reason to change things between us than her graduation. The spring is back in my step, and I skip every other stair, tackling the massive wooden staircase with newfound gusto. It creaks under the weight of my boots.

Arms crossed and stone-faced, Morgan's waiting to greet me at the top. He's not doing a damn thing to hide his contempt over whatever's bugged him all afternoon.

"You're not supposed to be up there when the girls are." Morgan grits his teeth.

"Came back down." My answer is nonchalant. I won't lie. I did come back down. After I came in his sister. I've walked by Morgan a dozen or more times on my way to see Cece. If she'd wanted to let the cat out of the bag, it was her choice. I'm not ruining it now out of frustration or to puff myself up. Not when my mind is made up about what role Celine has in my life and I want everyone else to treat her with the same respect.

She's mine. And my biggest problem is Morgan's forgotten he once trusted I'd never hurt his sister.

The scowl his ugly mug is sporting relaxes when Aidy wraps her arms around him from behind. "We're all ready!"

I haven't passed the last stair before the ladies turn me around. They slink their palms into their better halves', encouraging us across the street to Sweet Caroline's. A third, fifth—make that seventh wheel since Jasper, Hailey's boyfriend, has taken Skye's place —I wind up holding the doors for the couples as they march through with cheerful expressions.

"Where is Skye?" Hailey asks along the way.

"The caterer is dropping off the food in an hour. He offered to stay behind and wait," Carver supplies. "Trig's already inside with Kimber. He took off over there as soon as our meeting was over."

"And Kimber made sure Morgan wasn't on the schedule to bar back." Sloan smiles at her man while she chatters at the group.

"Why didn't anyone tell me why I had the night off?" Morgan quizzes his girlfriend. "It's my last opportunity to walk Celine home. What if I miss out on a sibling-bonding moment?"

"This was a need to know basis." Aidy teases him.

"She's my sister."

Aidy shrugs. "We had it under control."

"You enjoy having something to keep under wraps."

He moves her lavender highlighted hair behind her ear, pecking her on the cheek, and I'm fighting the green-eyed monster again. It doesn't bug me Morgan has Aidy, but that he's able to show affection toward her in front of everyone.

Meanwhile, at Sweet Caroline's front entrance, eighteen by twenty-four posters advertise Cece's farewell. In most of them she's clad in so little that the seductive way her arms cover her body gives the impression she's topless or buck-ass naked. I know inside these four walls the latter isn't true. Jake would lose his liquor license.

It's dark and noisy in the club. We have to push through the standing-room-only crowd that covers the path of twinkling floor lights to get to the booth Jake reserves for Carver. There's not much room for anyone else to sit if I do, so I pretend it's better for everyone else to have ample space. Reality is, I want to see Cees. If I take a spot at the table, nervous energy will have my leg bouncing it off the Richter scale.

Kimber's tending bar. She has Holly come take our

drink orders because Trig has her penned back there, aware it stops patrons from copping a feel. Holly's rockabilly style and short shorts attract the attention of an ass-grabbing guy nearby. I can't blame Trig for being overprotective of his wife and step forward, getting in the guy's face. The lascivious smile the bar's patron has plastered on fades and low-and-behold the dipshit is glowing white in the dark.

"Thanks, big guy." Holly motions over her shoulder at the creep. Her fingers dance up my bicep, but it means nothing to either of us. Holly's good people. She's got a kid at home and he's her number one priority. "What's your poison?"

"I'm drinking tonight." The nice thing about working here is the bartenders know your order, even if it's cryptic.

"Glad one of us is having fun," she remarks wryly. Holly's responsible for closing the place down when the rest of us clear out. A second dancer is on stage when she returns with a full tray of beer bottles, glasses, and the sometimes fruity, always non-alcoholic concoctions Kimber's perfected for anyone who needs a drink in their hand but has had addiction issues.

Time ticks slow when Carver lifts his pilsner in a toast. I get the sensation someone's pressed the pause button on my life and has forgotten to hit play. I guess the person was me.

"Oh, shit!" With an empty tray, Holly turns and puts her fingers to her lips, directing Kimber's attention to the table with an ear-piercing whistle. She points at Aidy and just like that everything speeds up.

Kimber opens a fridge, sliding a water bottle down the bar to Trig, who pitches it over the crowd. I catch it as the house lights dim to black, the music turns up, and strobe lights brighten the stage. When our eyes adjust, Aidy's drink is in front of her like magic.

It's the first time in hours Morgan's complimenting

my arm instead of shooting me a dirty look. But I don't have time to notice. Like me, the crowd is here to see Celine and they're going wild.

A lot of Jake's newer girls are into hardcore rap and techno. Cees mixes it up. Lately, she's been into sultry throwback singles. The crowd's demographic is skewed to men in their late thirties and early forties. This is the last music they heard before preschool television theme songs took over their playlists. She's smart enough to work their egos into a frenzy, with flashbacks of when they were studs instead of duds. Um, I mean dads.

The audience is sure when she shimmies off her shiny raincoat there won't be much underneath. I've seen this number before. Cece's pulled out a few stops from the *Intuition* video, including Jewel's short, slick red skirt with the loose yellow firefighter suspenders.

She reaches high to hang the coat from a hook, dragging her hands down the pole until she's bent in half and the skirt's ridden up to reveal a yellow plaid thong and the soft skin of her thighs that belongs to me.

I chuckle under my breath, wondering how much of a mess I left Celine to clean up. I'd hose her off now to see the tight wife-beater she has on soaked through. I'm enough of a man to admit I fantasize about Cece wearing clothes as much as her not wearing anything. It might be because it's a stretch to say she's dressed whenever we're in one another's company.

The music crescendos, booming louder. It's about to hit the note where Cece grabs the center of the shirt, ripping it in two. She lifts a leg high, prancing around the pole, and a man she's cautious when flirting with reaches out to touch the strappy boot tied up her calf. The strings come undone. It'll be tough to hit the marks on her footwork without falling after she tosses the tank into the crowd. Cece bends, making a coy show out of lacing the boot. It throws off her rhythm for half a beat, but she yanks the top in two and lands every mark.

Yet for me, before the songs even ended, the situation sent the needle scratching across the record with a screech. It's normal for customers to seek Cece's attention when she's out on the floor or by the bar. It also drives me up a fucking wall.

We had a blow-up about it a year ago when whatever it is we're doing first started. The disagreement is the most words we've spoken to one another. I was coming from Jake's office and saw a drunk guy getting handsy. The look of annoyance flashing across Cece's face got the best of me, and I interjected by clenching my fist around the guy's collar. Before I'd gone too far, Celine unwrapped my fingers from his shirt, comped the douche a drink on the house, and dragged my ass out the back door to the parking lot.

"I had it under control," she seethed, poking her manicured fingernail into my chest. "I can take care of myself." Her brown eyes were dark and stormy. "Do not overstep and pretend we are what we're not."

She didn't give me a chance to defend my actions, and I swear had I followed on her heels back into the building, lightning might've blinded me she was so furious.

But I was mad too. After that, I fucking sought her out until what we were doing was part of her routine and if I didn't appear in the bathroom for too many days in a row, she'd almost look at me across the bar as if she missed me.

This time she could have broken her ankle. Then what? Miss her party? Get her diploma on crutches?

For the second time in as many hours, I'm done with nobody knowing about us besides us. It is my problem. And I'm about to change that.

Chapter Four

Celine

I can hear the thump of music for the next performer through the walls, but the dressing room is quiet. Jake's insisted the dancers all be out on the floor tonight between sets. I have enough time to freshen up before joining them.

Sliding into the seat at my vanity, I pluck a few candid snapshots of me and the girls out of the mirror and study our smiles.

I almost don't remember a time when Kimber wasn't my boss and, while she and Sloan are a generation ahead of me, they're two of my closest friends because we lived at the mill together. It was weird when Kimber married Trig and he bought their house. It'll be stranger when I move out. I'm used to seeing one or the other of them every day.

I shuffle through the other pictures. Me and Aidy. God, I love that girl. She makes up for every damned thing my brother endured. Hailey, who I still can't believe is an adult when I'd first met her as a gawky teen. Holly, our assistant manager, and I making duck faces with our eyes rolled up. We weren't even drunk. Just being ridiculous on her first night solo without Kimber in charge or Jake pretending to pay attention to this place. They'd put every available person on the schedule to make sure nothing went wrong. I swear there were more employees here than customers. We had the best time.

These people, they're my family. I'm sad to leave. Sometimes coming to work—yes, and taking off my clothes—was a reprieve from the stress of studying. I lived for the moment, knowing the best ones are fleeting.

I have zero regrets about how I made my way in this life. It may have taken me longer to realize the dream, but it's within my grasp. I hadn't realized how bittersweet the end was.

Jake tried to convince me to stay on because I bring in a decent crowd of regulars he doesn't want to lose.

I harrumph. I saw one of the newer girls giving a guy who claims to be my biggest fan a lap dance earlier. She's got Jake's concerns covered. She also waved a Benjamin in my face and stopped griping that the last few nights weren't great for tips.

Jake put all his effort into advertising my big send-off all over the marquee. He wanted as many patrons as possible for my final show, and he got them. I've got to go on a few extra times, so I'm not expected to work the crowd long. Jake wants them hungry for more and too drunk to realize the cash they slip under my thong isn't from anything more indecent than a smile when I bat my eyelashes.

I'll give Jake credit there. His mom was an exotic dancer, and he doesn't expect us to do more than shimmy our hips entertaining customers. Although, he's never attempted to stop what goes on when the curtains are drawn in the small alcove of rooms beyond the stage.

I've done a few things in those rooms St. Peter will question me for at the pearly gates, but nothing promiscuous. Those pretend sexual favors, hovering in a man's lap, all took place in plain sight. The teasing became bothersome the more times I was with Dusty. I didn't want him to see me skirting the edges of men's fantasies. I don't sleep around and, whether or not my job evokes the perception I do, it's not one I want my friends having of me. Not to mention, the thought of touching another man, or letting him get close enough to take advantage of the way they want to touch me, is unappealing.

But is Dusty so attractive to me because he's off-limits?

I place the pictures to the side and study my reflection. I'm alone in a far corner. There's a second row of vanities blocking my view of the exit. I hear the door open and shut.

The man of the hour appears in between the aisle of mirrors. Standing stock-still, Dusty repeats his words from earlier when we were alone together at the mill. "Door's locked."

I nod.

He's immense next to the frilly boas and wigs, nail polish, and tubes of lipstick. In two strides he's crossed the room and is down on his knees. Mine spread of their own volition, cradling his body.

A warm hand pulls my hip toward him. Kneeling while I'm seated, Dusty and I are on eye level. His thumb caresses my cheek before taking my mouth in a demanding kiss. It's filled with as much hunger and sexual desire as any has ever been. I palm his hard cock through his jeans. This has never happened here, and my pulse is racing. I'm torn between unzipping his pants to spring it free, letting Dusty push my costume to the side, and doing what's right.

Sex has never been like this with any other man. Hot

and dirty. Combustible. And yet I've never once felt as if I was in danger. It's the complete opposite as if Dusty would blanket his body over mine like a shield. I'm not sure if the notion is real or imagined.

The stupid love-sick girl I haven't allowed myself to be since I was a moody teenager believes we're connected. The woman who freely gives her body to a man, not knowing if he'll show his face the next day, won't stop telling the stupid girl to protect her heart at all costs.

Dusty tugs at my lower lip, before diving his tongue back into my mouth lazy and slow. His hand hasn't moved from my jaw as he guides our actions into a kiss from him like I've never had.

It makes the sadness, the worries over my next steps in life, ebb away. This seems like a promise that I can seek him out.

"Do you want me?" I don't get turned on when I dance. But the last minute and a half has me dripping. We'd have a lot to explain if we got caught, but not nearly as much as someone walking in on us in the factory bathroom. I doubt either of us will bring it up. We're consenting adults. It's where we've been having sex that makes it wrong.

"Understatement." He chuckles. A broad grin stretches across his face.

I smile, wiping the smudge of red lipstick off his lower lip. It follows my fingers, kissing my palm. The intense look he's giving me is a far cry from the stern one I'm used to seeing. Dusty's normal intent is in making my body come alive. Now? He's—happy? I should know, but I'm not sure. His expression's not as brooding and intense.

I tilt his chin and bring his lips back to mine. Our teeth scrape as I giggle. Dusty wraps his arms around me and I wrap my legs around him. However, he's not taking it further.

"What's wrong?" I ask.

"Wanna take you out."

"What? Where?" My nose scrunches and a heated blush rises from my chest. "I'm not exactly dressed for the occasion in this and, with the party later, it's not like I can escape to the Wafflehaus after my shift."

"Royce's."

I blink fast. Royce's is an upscale restaurant. A place you have to make reservations well in advance. It has a dress code. The appetizer alone will cost a fortune.

Dusty wants to take me on a date. There are two things I know about a man who throws around scads of cash on a single meal with a woman. *Their first meal together.* Either the woman is prostituting herself for Chateaubriand and a hundred dollar bottle of wine or the man is serious about her.

Given Dusty's already getting the milk for free, he's not in a position to buy the cow. I can only presume he's serious about *me*.

I swallow hard to stop the love-sick teenager from screaming "Yes!" like she did in the backseat after her Prom.

Dusty watches my reactions as I lick my lips and breathe out.

We're not... Fucking is not a reason to go on a date. I'm stalling with my answer. As much as teenage me wants to achieve the sense of euphoria I've denied myself, I'm petrified of what happens when our friends see us together. They'll think Dusty's interested in a relationship with the prefixes "girl" and "boy" before friend. That isn't us. I'm not sure I'm at a point in my life where I'm ready for that.

You're a bitch, Cece Wescott. You know what you aren't ready for. Admit your misgivings. Admit how dating this man would make you feel when it's not his cock thrusting into you that counts, but being responsible for his heart.

Would it be so bad if we kept what's happened

between us to ourselves? It's bound to peter out and who wants to explain why we didn't work as a couple when we weren't one in the first place.

Dusty's thumb makes gentle circles at my side. "Graduation. Rroyce's to celebrate. You and me. My gift to you."

"Okay." I hoping my squeak doesn't sound terrified.

I don't want to hurt Dusty. His offer is so sincere. All the guys have free-flowing cash. He's being nice. Men do this for their cum dumpsters all the time, right? I shouldn't read into it. I also shouldn't refer to myself as Dusty's cum dumpster, but the phrase has stopped me from searching for any underlying meaning in what we've done.

"Um, I'm busy the next few weeks. There's the actual graduation ceremony. Christmas. Then I start at the clinic. Also, I offered to stay with Owen at Kimber and Trig's to watch him because Morgan and Aidy are going on vacation with them over New Year's." I rattle on like I'm a social butterfly instead of the girl whose friends drag her into Raleigh kicking and screaming.

"Af-ter the New Year. When you're settled…and can tell me about it all." The bulbs in my mirror highlight the gold flecks in his brown eyes.

Dusty stands without kissing me. He's never said goodbye so, when the door closes behind him, I'm not sure why my lady bits are disappointed. Oh, well, yeah. *Now I get it.* But the rest? It bugs the hell out of me to the point of irritation.

He scratches an itch and maybe I hadn't read into his intentions because I hadn't wanted to admit mine were shallow. Perhaps because delving deeper isn't where I saw my life heading. The challenges of finishing my degree and getting accepted into the PA program were my focus. Being sidetracked by men and having kids the way my friends are would put a damper on chasing my goals.

My family is a shitshow. My mother's pregnancy with me and my brother being born so soon after trapped her. We had less than half of what most families did. Yet, without all the sweetness we saw others growing up with, somehow Morgan and I learned how to turn lemons into lemonade.

I slip a robe over my shoulders, cinching it in the middle, and pulling at the lapels. The silky fabric drapes over my costume, exposing ample cleavage.

Swinging the door wide and stepping into the hall, the sole of my boot snags on loose carpeting. This is the second time tonight it causes a malfunction. Dusty is leaning against the wall out in the hallway. His thick arms rest over his broad chest and he has his legs crossed. He catches me as I stumble.

"Were you waiting for me?"

"Fix that tomorrow," he says, putting me back on my feet.

I fake a smile, ignoring the blood rushing to my ears and thud of my pulse. I turn on my heel toward the bar, making eye contact with Holly. There's got to be as much heat radiating from my cheeks as is coming off Dusty's palm, a mere inch from my back.

Reaching the end of the hall, I make an excuse about getting a drink. Increasing my stride, I hope no one at the table full of my friends notices Dusty is behind me. In my peripheral vision, he veers off toward them.

Holly's filling a glass with club soda. When she looks up her eyes widen. Without skipping a beat, she places the drink on the bar.

"I like that shade. It is new?" She rubs under her lower lip and strikes me I hadn't checked my appearance in the mirror. "I swear even the best ones are never smudge-proof."

Oh, damn. My jaw drops. I rub at my mouth, messing my lipstick up even more. There's not a brand I've bought capable of surviving the way Dusty kisses me.

Celine

Holly grabs my chin, dipping a napkin into the tonic and wiping the stain away. "Go get 'em," she says when she's all done fixing my face.

She looks over my shoulder in the opposite direction and I follow her gaze. Most of the crowd is intent on watching the act on stage, but there are at least half a dozen guests who have me in their sights and the reason Jake has me out here is to cater to them.

I chose a couple to approach who'll do me the most good. Yes, couple. She's blonde and her partner is a brunette. They've been here before and my interactions with them have been pleasant, which is saying a lot given the number of crotch-grabbers I deal with.

With a wide grin, I strut across the room to the two-person table they're seated Fit to thank them for coming. The blonde's palm caresses the bell of my hip and I lean over, letting my breasts spill out of the robe so her girlfriend gets the better view, air-kissing both of the woman's cheeks. A shrill whistle and lewd catcall from the table next to theirs isn't worth acknowledging.

Truth is, it's helping me do what I'm supposed to: get a bunch of horny guys amped up. I hate to call men predictable, however, I haven't encountered one yet who doesn't have a threesome with two women or fantasy with lesbians playing into it somehow. This show I'm putting on is as gratifying for them as it is watching me on stage. They'll wind up panting during my next performance and buying more alcohol to quench their thirst.

In spite of the occasional hand roaming over my robe or the bare skin of my thigh, it's incredible how respectful the ladies I'm entertaining right now are. I get this is their idea of fun. They might be the sort to take me home to play out a few of their own fantasies, or maybe they wouldn't and they use my performances to enhance whatever happens between the two of them later on. Those predilections aren't any of my nevermind.

What is my business is keeping customers happy in the here and now, and it's easy to accomplish when, as a woman, I understand a little attention from someone you find attractive goes a long way.

Since this is my night, I'm relishing the low-pressure of this couple. Not to mention, my back is to Carver's booth and I can forget for a few minutes what led to the lipstick faux pas.

The owner is working the room too. Jake fakes his interest in Sweet Caroline's well when he has to, if it adds to his bottom line.

The brunette sticks her hand up under my robe, tucking a tip at my waistband. I make a production of winking and thanking her.

"Aren't you generous?" The owner slips into our conversation. Jake towers over me and I'm not short without these heels on. His frosty blue eyes should be a dead giveaway to what's trapped within his soul. Yet, most women are certain all the Icelandic God needs to change is some platinum pussy.

"We are." Based on her response, I guess the brunette is up to the challenge. She licks her lips, and her partner touches Jake's tailored black slacks the way she had me when we'd begun talking.

"Celine is needed backstage. How about a *private* tour behind the scenes and a round *on* the house for your troubles?" He procures a bold "reserved" tepee from his breast pocket, placing it down as the two women rise from their seats.

I scoot off, trying not to gag. Jake's taking my intent of amping up the guests one step further with a detour to his office. I'd be surprised if one of them doesn't have his dick in her mouth while her partner gets spread out on his desk. Unless they get off on having men watch. Again, this is a sex club, so other's proclivities aren't mine to judge.

Fucking Jake is a line I've never crossed and the idea of him using me to get his jollies hadn't entered my mind. Not like this anyway. I'm not disgusted by his actions. Okay, I am. But I'll get over it since this is the last night I have to work the floor. Next time I'm at Sweet Caroline's it's to hang out the way my friends are doing over at Carver's table. So caught up in enjoying themselves, they're not even paying attention to the act.

Heading over there, I know I'll want to forget my next set and all of the patrons here to see me. For the moment, I'd let it slide that Dusty is with them. I hesitate to look over there so I don't see him watching me.

My attention drifts to the bar as I move through the crowd, and I'm shocked. Dusty's back is to everyone. He's engaged in a close discussion with Holly. Her tits with pert nipples rest on the counter. I've never cared braless was part of Holly's charm until Dusty chuckles and his head lowers to the over-polished wood she normally buffs with a rag and not her boobs.

The confidence that I'm the only cow Dusty's getting the milk from evaporates. I have half a mind to march over there and sling my arm over Dusty's shoulder to gauge Holly's reaction. I can understand why she'd want him and only stop myself because she's never been a miserable crotch to me. Holly's exceptional at her job and has a mouth to feed at home. I won't start a catfight with her. She doesn't need trouble on her doorstep and, on a packed night like tonight, whatever I do is bound to cause a scene.

She's probably the one Dusty wants anyhow. Holly doesn't take off her clothes for her paycheck. Her style is unique while the rest of us here dress plain old slutty for our tips. Dusty's offer to take me to Royce's? It's a thank you, right? He's feeding me a steak and kicking me to the curb. I won't be around anyhow. I'm moving out, he's moving on.

Sneaking back into the dressing room, I change into a one-piece black leather number for my second time on stage. It matches the boots and pasties I'm wearing. This costume is a bitch to put on and I would've sweated like a pig out on the floor. The pasties slip through wide cut outs in the bustier. I consider taking them off. Plenty of other girls go topless. As long as we're not completely nude, no one's calling the health inspector. Who am I kidding? No one cares enough anyhow. I've left my barest parts to everyone else's imagination. The only reason I'm contemplating this is to get a rise out of a man who needs no provocation. Dusty's hard as nails each time we're together. I try to tell myself we're all adults here, so let's call a spade a spade and be done with it... All the while part of me wants to schedule a vet appointment to get the man neutered.

On stage, I sway to the haunting music. This is one of my favorite dances. I know it by heart. Kimber helped choreograph it, and I involuntarily sink down on my knees and sway back up when I listen to the song in my room at the mill. I could perform this number in my sleep and my mind wanders off.

I can't see Dusty, but—like the nights I've pretended to dance only for him to find him holding up a wall as the house lights come up—he's here. Don't ask me how my body knows to react to his presence. It's been like a chemical reaction from the get-go.

I ball change before strutting forward, my toes pointing in my tightly laced boots, remembering how surprised I was when Dusty told me Morgan had asked him to walk me across the street to the mill.

He was quiet, and I felt a bit of a fool for trying to pry open his clamped jaw, peppering him with questions that left me with few answers. The thick air was charged with an uncomfortable silence and I shivered with anticipation, waiting for those clipped responses.

Dusty had his toolbox in one hand and a bucket filled with an auger and rags in the other. At the point we should have gone our separate ways, I'd veered from the landscaped path to the front door and followed Dusty to the parking lot behind the building. He opened the rear driver's door to his quad cab, putting his tools on the floor. I leaned my hip into the frame. The door snicked shut and Dusty looked at me as if something was in his way.

When his hand yanked me away from his truck, I realized it was me. Yet, when his mouth descended on mine in a blinding kiss, his reasons for needing me to move differed from what I'd suspected.

His large palm caught in my hair as our lips crushed together. The connection I'd felt? He'd sensed it too. And, damn, if I didn't tip up on my toes when Dusty pulled away.

I heard a rumble in the distance and lightning flashed across the sky, rattling my bones.

"I shouldn't have..." His sentence trailed, but he'd spoken as I was about to combust waiting for Dusty to say something, anything.

I rolled my bottom lip between my teeth. The taste of him lingered and my tongue shot out, seeking the remains.

Dusty lowered his mouth to my ear. "More?"

One word full of meaning. *Did I want more?* Hell, I was ready to let this man give me every hard inch of him. My nails dug into his forearms. I racked my brain trying to find the nearest location without security cameras to hide us from view. Although, I doubted we'd give anyone a show inside the truck.

Another roaring rumble caught my attention coming from the back lot entrance. Skye rode in on his motorcycle. A tiny droplet wet my shirt.

Dusty hit his key fob so the headlights turned on, illuminating the darker spot where we stood.

Skye noticed us, swaggering over with a triumphant grin. "Beat the rain. What're you doing out here?"

I pushed past Dusty, agitated at the cold water dumped on my head. "You and your bike. You're going to get yourselves killed trying to outrun raindrops." Skye, Jasper, and Trig are forever telling stories of waiting out spring and summer deluges under an overpass.

I followed Skye to the factory's rear entrance, sneaking a glance back at the massive man silhouetted by the headlights. My smile and the shake of my hips should have ensured he understood he was welcome to tag along. But to my dismay, Dusty doesn't make another move for weeks until after he's gone all alpha-male at the club. I told him off and within twenty-four hours we're picking up in the bathroom right where we'd left off in the parking lot. The build-up to it made me hotter than sin and, no matter how many times I've fucked him since, that afternoon is still some of the best sex I've ever had.

The way it's supposed to, my body drops in mock submission to the final note of the song. My third time on stage is over. The rest of the night's been a blur. Like the second act before it, I've gone through the motions, using the music to reflect on where Dusty and I started and what he wants from me. I've experienced every emotion in the course of a few hours, from confusion and anger through childlike hope. It's left me wound tight. Despite the way my body has swayed, I'm a knotted ball of nerves.

The crowd whistles and hollers. Jake gets up on stage. He hugs me as if he's hugged me before and says a few words. More to get the crowd to come back again than bidding me farewell.

I lallygag, joking with the other dancers in the dressing room. Morgan is waiting for me when I step out into the brightly lit theater. The cleaning crew is vacuuming the carpet and the bouncers and waitstaff are heading out. My heart skips a beat seeing Dusty behind the bar helping Holly restock.

"Was he bothering you tonight?"

I must've craned my neck trying to get one last glimpse of Dusty. My facial muscles, tight from plastering happiness across them, have drawn into a frown. My discontent is apparent even to me.

"No. Only tired," I lie. My brother had asked me something similar long enough ago that I'm hoping he doesn't tie the two events together. Besides, it doesn't matter if Dusty's moving on to greener pastures. I am too.

"Well, I'm sure your party will perk you up." Morgan's over-enthusiastic tugging me out of the front entrance.

"I guess it will."

But it doesn't because Dusty never shows.

Chapter Six

Celine

"Ooh! This would look fantastic on you, Cece!"

I pull a gray sweater over a pink sleeveless top and pop my head above the slatted dressing room door to see what Sloan's gushing over.

It's mill girls' day. Something that, between Christmas shopping and January sales, has become an even more frequent occurrence, mostly because everyone's schedules are so varied it's been hard for us all to get together at once. Last weekend, Hailey enticed me with breakfast and fresh produce shopping. Only Aidy could join us at the Farmer's Market. Today, Hay is on a ride with Jasper and Aidy's working at Baked Beans, Brighton's downtown village coffee shop and bakery next to this boutique.

Carver and Trig are pressing the flesh with Jake on the links. I don't care if we live in North Carolina. What sane person golfs in January? Kimber was the manager on duty at Sweet Caroline's last night, but took full advantage of her hubby being gone for the day. She hasn't taken her sunglasses off inside and is nursing her second espresso. With her feet propped on an ottoman in the changing area, if I didn't know any better, I'd think she'd played a few rounds at the nineteenth hole before noon. However, Kimber is a recovering addict, and she's bleary-eyed from being up early to care for her baby and drop him off south of Raleigh at Aidy's adoptive parents', Don and Ghillie Fairley, for the day.

Though they resemble and act more like sisters, Kimber is my brother's girlfriend's biological mother. The Fairleys are an older couple and, smitten with Owen, they treat him like he's their grandson. I'm happy Morgan's part of this extended family. Although when the Fairleys are around, I'm the odd man out. So someday I hope to have a similar situation too. Until then, my mill girls are more than sufficient.

"Where would I wear a dress to?" I open the door to the changing room, drawn to the vibrant silky red fabric. I rub it between my fingertips, admiring the intricate lace collar, and the desire to buy it ratchets up. It's not practical, though. There are six other items I've had my eye on, all of which complete a work ensemble. I may purchase two or three of them. Before shopping today, I'd struck a deal with myself to only buy professional clothes. I didn't even get anything new for my graduation since the cap and gown hid the skirt I'd worn that afternoon.

Sloan holds the dress up in the air, then to the front of me. She quirks a brow and moves back to the side, inspecting the outfit with price tags still attached that I'm trying on. She lets out a low whistle. "All you need is some horn-rimmed glasses and an Annie Lennox song and you could make the cash back to pay for both of these."

I finger the lace top again before putting the dress back on the rack. "I wish I'd seen this before New Year's."

"Because you would have looked great all dolled up

for my toddler," Kimber removes her shades. "This is stunning." She motions to my current ensemble. "The dress is too. When are you going to stop dating a spoon and a half gallon of vanilla? Love her to death, but a Sandra Bullock movie and ice cream is not what they mean by 'Netflix and chill'."

I shrink when Sloan gets in on the act, reminding me how many times she drags me downstairs in a week.

Kimber hugs me. "You gotta come out of your shell sometime. I swear, girl. In the last year, you've gone from hardly a date to not seeing anyone at all."

"We get school was important—" Sloan pipes up.

"But are you living your best life?" Kimber finishes.

I don't have an answer. The way they make it sound, I'm not. But I haven't worked in pediatrics long enough for the ink on my diploma to have dried. Are there steps between steps to reach goals I don't know about? I won't let my face fall in disappointment. What I'm hearing is "you need a man" and yet, they're unaware I've had one. Sort of, anyway.

Except, Dusty and I weren't much and when he decided it was over, I did too.

A bell jingles a tinkly tune in the store. "I'm here!" Holly calls. "Hold on. No, I'm not." She gets sidetracked by a different dress near the window with a wide belt.

She holds it up for us to approve. We all shake our heads no. Holly's got great taste in clothes all-around, but the candy apple classic style is her own and not everything she's attracted to matches the retro look she sticks to. The rest of us couldn't get away with dressing the way she does unless it was Halloween.

She gives the garment one last glance in a long mirror and decides, "Nope. You're right. Not me," and joins our group of three. Instead of a real hello, she signals the tags at my wrist. "If nobody's told you yet, buy that."

I head back into the changing room since now that Holly's here, and apparently the number one complaint they have about my life is being manless, Dusty is in the forefront of my mind.

At first, I all-out avoided the man. I was mad he hadn't shown for the party. I may not have planned to spend the rest of the night with him by my side, but when Dusty paid more attention to Holly than me, I became mistrustful. Yes, even if I'd sought to avoid him after he asked me out. But most of all, I was mad at myself for not being able to handle my emotions. I still am.

The holidays were a distraction, but as I count the days, it's been a month since quitting the club. I haven't seen hide nor hair of Dusty, even when I've heard a sound reminding me of him and ducked out of my room to look down the hall. He hadn't shown at Carver's Christmas Eve party. And where I began working at the medical office park right after the New Year, it's not as if he could drop by to see me while I was getting ready for Sweet Caroline's. My grown-up job doesn't have the same hours the one in adult entertainment did. We aren't even ships passing in the night.

I change back into my street clothes, decide to only get the cardigan, and then change my mind when I realize it was Holly's opinion which made me not want the top. I'd be cutting off my nose to spite my face, not getting something I wanted because she liked it. The women here have more experience with men, but I'm smart enough to understand it's a man coming between my friendship with her. A man I want, for all the wrong reasons, and she's got.

In all likelihood, they have more in common. Dusty's age lands squarely between ours. My brother is younger than me, but even he's getting to the point where he's done with women who are still trying to find themselves and is in a steady relationship.

Stepping back out, Sloan's paying for her armful of purchases and Kimber's snoozing in the chaise, waiting for us to check out.

"You're not getting anything?"

She holds up a tiny bag, so I presume its earrings or jewelry.

Holly's browsing my favorite display of perfumes and lotions. She twists the lid on a bottle and sniffs. "This smells pretty." Her nose wiggles, taking a second whiff. "And familiar. Hey, Cece, do you wear this?"

I sidle up next to her, reaching for a different container of bath beads to see if I like the scent. "I bought the lemon and basil gift set before the holidays." It was a token Christmas present from me to me. Something I started doing when I got a steadier income. "Before this store stocked it, I used the watermelon and mint. It's a lot lighter on your skin. I like how the lemon lingers, but you don't reek of bathing in floor wax and it's not a sticky pink lemonade odor. It's—"

"Clean and fresh." She puts a dab from the tester on her wrist.

"Yeah," I agree when she offers the bottle labeled coconut and hibiscus to me to pump.

I'm torn, wanting to confess I've slept with Dusty. It's better if she finds out from me rather than getting so far into a relationship with him that keeping it from her makes Holly hurt or angry. But this horrible part of me is jealous, and I can't help hoping whatever is between Holly and Dusty isn't serious.

I lift the spot I've dabbed to my nose. The coconut is smooth. The hibiscus is overpowering for my taste. More perfumy than refreshing.

"What did you find?" Kimber noses in. "Are we going to see Aidy?"

"Did your espresso kick in, Dearest?" Holly counters the two swift questions with a pat on the arm.

"Yes, finally."

"How long until your next dose?"

"You're awful."

"Oh, I'm awful? Come here, let me hug you! Have you ever worked with you when you are caffeine-free? I'm terrorized by the idea of Owen becoming a big brother. Nine months of you and decaf at midnight and I'm jumping up and down when Jake drags his sorry ass into the club." Holly's the first to pull out of the embrace.

"Say what you mean, why don't you?" Kimber strokes her long red hair back behind her shoulders, her sunglasses now a makeshift headband.

"You know I will. I love you so much, I'll even buy your next grande."

They both snicker at the deal, secure in the rapport they keep.

I wish I had the confidence to tell my friends anything. If it's serious between them, Holly wouldn't care about his slow speech or get her feathers ruffled by anyone questioning her interest in him beyond the physical.

If I'd been smart, I might have asked Holly's advice about Dusty. Or even said to Kimber or Sloan, "Hey, there's this guy..." Now I've dug too deep a hole to climb out of.

In our group, everybody's got somebody and the body I had was never mine to begin with.

My imagination plays tricks on me. I envision Dusty dropping his nose to nuzzle behind Holly's ear, the way he's done to me. I wonder if she'd say I helped her pick out the scent. If he'd react at all hearing my name. I worry he might prefer hibiscus to lemon.

The moment I shut my heart off years ago comes back vividly. It's accompanied by other memories, like accepting a date with a boy attractive enough to have sex with, but I'd leave behind before they dragged me down. My only real experiences with romantic love are watching people use the word to cause pain.

I offer for the girls to go next door to Baked Beans, saying I'll be there as soon as the salesclerk has cashed me out. Sloan and Kimber take me up on it. To my chagrin, Holly stays put.

"What with the glum face?" She tsks, a crooked smile on her flawless painted red lips. Her purchases are bagged. She's cheery, popping a fresh bottle of lemon basil lotion on top of my pile of clothes. "Trust me. It's perfect on you."

Something stabs in my heart. If his intentions were honest, I think I'm the one who hurt Dusty. That's why he hasn't come back. Why he's ready to move on with Holly.

I finish paying for my purchases. My stomach is in knots, and I don't know if I'm green with envy or coming down with an attack of conscience. Either way, if I open my mouth now, I'll wreck the day. "Could you tell Sloan and Kimber I'm going home? I'm not feeling well."

"Sure thing." She loops an arm in mine, guiding me out of the store. "When you're better, we need to chat about a condo being rented near me."

"Okay," I squeak. I'm having a hard enough time letting go of him now. How can I ever live in the same complex as Holly does if Dusty's around?

Chapter Seven

Celine

I wrap my stethoscope around my neck. "Everything checks out fine. If you don't have any more questions, the nurse will be back in a few minutes."

The little girl sitting on the exam table shakes her head. She's been swinging her knees back and forth since I tapped them with the triangular tipped rubber hammer. Annoyed, her father has been trying to silence the methodical banging her heels make against the steel drawers.

"One last thing, I saw we have all new stickers up at the checkout desk so make sure you snag one of those." I point at my lapel. I hadn't been able to resist a shimmery fish sticker when the receptionist unboxed them. It was a coup because the infant in for his six-month check-up before I saw this patient had become mesmerized by the colorful scales during the exam. I may change up my sticker every week.

The girl oohs and aahs, and I tell her there are others like it. She should choose two. She may have a sibling. I'd had two cavities filled as a child. It earned me an extra treasure chest prize, and I selected one Morgan was thrilled to get.

"If you don't mind me asking, have we met before? You look familiar," her dad asks, helping his daughter jump down while I scrub up.

I don't have the heart to mention getting off the exam table is pointless. She needs shots at this physical. There was a mom here last week irate over the charges for a second appointment. Her husband had walked out of his son's preventive care exam without following her checklist. I wasn't sure what was more surprising; a wife making a list, a husband needing one, or the idea the second trip in to see a provider was free. Then again, I'm learning as much now about nuances of healthcare administration as I did about medicine when I was in the PA program.

"I don't think so. I've only been at this clinic for a few weeks. Not long enough to forget a face yet." I blow off his insistence we've met.

This has happened to me before. For all we know, he pulled his vehicle in alongside the next pump over during a recent fill-up at the gas station. I have no reason to jog his memory. The inclination to do so means I'm stuck here longer. My feet are more tired from standing all day than they ever were dancing in stilettos. Thank goodness it's almost quitting time.

With his daughter distracted, I grimace and point at my upper arm, mouthing, "shots".

He gets the wide-eyed aha look at my gesture and turns to distract her.

I scoot out of the tiny room, handing the notes I've taken over to Gloria who is organizing files behind the nurses' station. "Last one of the day."

"Oh, yay!" She sounds enthused, then her lip curls. "You gave me shots at four forty-five in the afternoon? On a Friday no less. Some warning would have been nice."

"I didn't know until I got in the exam room." I shrug. "But I'll make it up to you. One of my girls, Aidy, works at Baked Beans. She swears they make the best chocolate-filled croissants. I'll bring you one on Monday morning to make up for it."

"Deal." Gloria spins on her heel toward the supply room where the locked cabinets holding injections are.

"Hey," I call after her. "She's got a rainbow on her shirt."

Gloria walks back holding up what I know are tie-dyed bandages we stock for teens. "This is the third time this week. I'm getting smart to you, but what happens when we run out of these."

"Everybody loves Tweety Bird?"

Gloria pauses with her hand on the knob of the exam room door. "They do not. They love Scooby-Doo bandages and getting Sylvester the Cat is worse than the shots."

I laugh. I like Gloria. She's in her mid-forties and is quick to speak her mind. With sons in high school at home, she insists there's no reason to mince words. Teenagers have a similar attention span to a fruit fly.

Gathering my things to leave, I wince hearing the little girl cry. While I'll always feel bad, Gloria says I'll get over the reaction. Right now, I'm sorry she has to deal with it. But: croissant.

Checking my cell, it has several missed calls from Sloan and group chats between the mill girls trying to coordinate a day we can all go out on the town. Without Hailey, Aidy stuck behind the bakery counter, and me scooting off with my tail between my legs, last weekend didn't count.

I pull my coat around my shoulders. The sun is still rising late and setting early. It's cold out there, and the thought of a breeze sends chills down my back. One of my favorite things about North Carolina are days when the wintertime temperature lands squarely in the mid-eighties. It's a pleasant reminder the sultry summer is on its way. We're in desperate need of one soon.

I say goodbye to the clinic's receptionist and open the heavy wooden door to the lobby, engrossed in my cell the way people shouldn't be when driving. It swings wide and I plow right into something solid. I swear my entire body reverberates like I've hit a gong. Even my inner ear is ringing.

About to lose my footing, a thick palm wraps over the dark fabric of my coat. "Whoa." The gravelly baritone husk floods my body with instant awareness.

"Dusty, what are you doing here?" Does my voice give away my excitement? God, I hope it doesn't. I sound desperate if it does.

He lets go of my arm when I'm secure on two feet and looks at me almost as if he doesn't know me. I stare down at my clothes. My pants are pressed. My button-up shirt leaves *everything* to the imagination compared to what I've slinked around in in the past. These new clothes are pretty and demure. Professional. I feel good about myself and yet self-conscious as Dusty takes me in. I'm concerned he doesn't like what he sees. Our eyes meet and his lip twitches as if he has a secret.

I tuck a strand of hair behind my ear that's come undone from a side braid and worry my lip. No longer concerned it's cold outside, I can feel my cheeks tingle pink while I wait for his response.

"Neurology." He throws a thumb over his shoulder, the thick sweater he has on bunches at his bicep.

I miss those arms.

"Oh, I'm sorry." I stammer. "It's none of my business."

"It's okay. Check-up. Clean bill of health." He holds up a folded sheet of printer paper I recognize as an invoice. "With a bill to clean out my wallet."

I laugh. "Medical care is expensive. Do you have to go a lot?"

"Not anymore." He takes a deep breath, his chest heaving. "You headed home?"

I nod.

"Walk you to your car?"

I peep my agreement.

Dusty holds the glass door open, letting me go first. We step into the cold parking lot. Crossing to the next row is hardly far enough to go to get over the uncomfortable silence before I say, "This is me. Dusty —"

"Cece—"

Each of us tries to speak at once. I titter again and Dusty's cheeks bunch into a wide grin. God, he's handsome. My hands ball in my pocket to stop from reaching up to touch the scruff of his beard and pull his lips close to mine.

"Nice to see you again." Dusty hasn't looked at me since we got outside. He turns to go and my fingers blatantly disregard the signals from my brain and catch his forearm.

"Hey, um." How do I ask this without seeming like all I'm interested in as a free meal? "Did you still want to get together? To ah, celebrate?" My hands fly in the air and the strap of my bag slips down my arm. Dusty's thick, calloused fingers put it back in place.

He glances around the lot, including through the rearview window of my vehicle. Anywhere but at me.

"You're not inter-ested."

"What? I didn't say that."

"Gave me lots of excuses, Cees." His eyes finally find mine again, boring into me with the truth we're both well aware of.

I did make up reasons to push it off. Frankly, I'm still uncertain of why I'd want to go. I don't know where I stand in his life, and I'm petrified of what I mean to this man. I've read into so many of his actions. Was I more than a fling? I won't be ready for a serious relationship until I'm established in my career and no one can drag me down to the depths my mother found herself in. But I can't lie. I miss this man.

I recognize the possibility I miss the sex. What we had can't go on the way it was, now can it? So, perhaps we have to go about it in a different manner.

"I'm sorry." I wince, grabbing the bag's strap to keep my hands occupied. "You didn't show up later at the party."

Dusty's palms glide back in his hair. He rests them behind his head. "Yeah, well." His expression sours.

I watch him search for words. Yet, those that come take me off guard.

"Your brother was being an ass."

"Morgan? What had his boxers in a bunch?" He'd seemed happy enough to me since he never wanted me stripping to begin with.

"He'd seen us walk out of the hallway... You sprinted away from me."

"I didn't run."

"Hardly touched you, Cees. You bolted. Then Morgan won't let it rest. Paints a clear picture."

My hackles raise. "So you're sticking your dick in Holly now?" *Wow, spiteful much?*

"What? No." Dusty's taken aback. This is the fastest I've heard him respond to anyone. "What makes you think anything is going on between Holly?"

In the rush to defend himself, I have to extrapolate the meaning in Dusty's second sentence. I hear him forget words a lot when he talks to others. It's a sign of an underlying neurological condition and why, before we were ever together, I was patient letting him speak.

"You were with her the rest of the night and never showed up when everyone expected you to be at the mill."

"I got the fuck away from your brother so I didn't punch him. Embarrass you. Holly needed help. It got her home for her son faster. Everyone ditched out on their responsibili-ties to go to *your* party."

"Oh."

Dusty's lips flatten to a line. He lets me mull over how selfish I've acted. "Yeah, oh," he repeats as it sinks in. "Listen, Cees." Dusty scrubs his jaw. "Still want to take you out. But I don't have the energy for this shit. You're either in or you're out."

"I'm in." The words jump from my throat.

Chapter Eight

Dusty

She's in, I've been repeating in my head. The problem is, I'm fidgeting with my tie, wondering what I've gotten *myself* in for.

We fuck. Okay, that should be past tense: *We fucked* and I should've left that well enough alone.

I roll my shoulders, trying to get the collar of my dress shirt to loosen. In the past hour, I've had the creeping sensation I should have told Cece to forget about it, gotten mad when she accused me of screwing Holly, and used her attitude problem as a clean break. As if the night of her last performance hadn't been clean enough.

But in my mind, it's doubtless Cece is a woman who makes a man give up his thirty-day chip over and over again until he can beat his addiction. She's smart, sexy…elusive. The last part's gotta be it. The more Celine slips through my fingers, the more I want her. Tonight's the litmus test to see if having her attention for a few hours is what I expect it's supposed to be.

Landing reservations at Royce's was easier than

expected. It's been five days since running into her at the clinic and each of the past fucking four of them it's been a struggle to not show my face at the mill knowing she's home for the night. Avoiding Cece this month was a challenge I was successful navigating. She still posts her schedule, and I knew when it was safe for me to be at the factory without her there.

See me struggling not to wave the white flag in surrender to the drug that is her pussy? I didn't even want to be in it. Just close enough to smell it. To know it was mine for the taking. I don't even expect she'll want sex. It's not the reason I asked her out. If this is more, it's more. If being around Celine when we're both dressed puts a damper on things then I guess I've had it wrong this whole time.

Falling back into the apprehension I had when I told Cece about the reservation, I unknot the tie, repeating the process—complete with shoulder roll.

I figured she'd hedge this time the way she had when I first brought up taking her out. Instead, she agreed right off the bat to a weeknight, though the phone conversation lasted shorter than I'd hoped. Maybe because she stunned me stupid when she didn't give me a sorry excuse.

With T-Minus to go until I'm picking her up, my confidence has wavered and I'm dumbfounded she hasn't canceled. Luckily, the girl who I usually have a standing date with tonight is all about getting dressed up and having me take her someplace nice. The reservations wouldn't go to waste.

The third time is a charm and I slide my suit jacket over my ham-hock biceps, inspecting my appearance in Jake's office bathroom's mirror. It made more sense to get ready here. Jake's not around and Sweet Caroline's is a ghost town this early in the evening.

I stride out and down the hall. Holly pops up from behind the bar, shaking out a fresh rag and wipes up a spill in an "I'm a parent. I got this." no-nonsense fashion.

"Sweet Baby Jesus—Look at you!" She jumps. The two victory rolls shellacked on her head with enough hairspray to do serious environmental damage don't budge. "Where are you going?"

"Roy-ce's." The word gets stuck halfway and my palms get clammy.

"Ooh, fancy. No wonder you're all decked out."

Holly's about to ask who I'm taking when the phone rings. She answers, holding up a finger. I give her a minute. She tells the caller to hold on. "Have a marvelous time, Hon. But before I forget, it's still a go for you taking Bhodi next Tuesday?"

I give her a thumbs up. Tuesday is Holly's night off and her sister's kid is at her ex's. It's not often Holly asks for help, but I get how much easier it is to have someone you can count on. Her son, Bhodi, is a great kid and Renata likes the distraction Bhodi provides when he's around.

I lean my weight into the front door. Stepping out into the parking lot in a slick suit and expensive pair of shoes, I feel like the Macy's Day Parade version of Carver. I'm missing the sleek trademark sedan, but my truck's no jalopy. I had it washed, waxed, and vacuumed at the dealership's detail shop when I went to have the oil changed yesterday.

About to hoist myself up to climb in, Cece catches my attention running on her toes in high heels across the main street that bisects the cotton mill and the club. She has on a long gray coat contrasting the red of those shoes in the streetlight. Getting to the sidewalk, she notices me standing there and smiles.

"Thought I was picking you up." It's more of a statement. I'm glad to see her either way.

"I was ready early and saw your truck out the window."

Cees comes to a standstill in front of me. I'm looking down into her pretty brown eyes. She blushes when I don't talk and does the lip lick thing that goes right to my groin.

"Help you in?" I find my tongue only to lose it again when she replies, "Sure."

Around the other side of the cab, I open the door and have to lift Cece in. Seated, her knees peek out from under the gray coat. My hand involuntarily brushes between them when I see more red fabric from the skirt of whatever she's wearing underneath. I'm tempted to unbutton her coat. It took me off guard when she'd swung the door into me leaving work. She was almost unrecognizable and maybe even sexier because of the way her clothes hid all the parts of her I'm familiar with.

Her fingertips graze my trimmed beard before she reaches for the seatbelt. Cece feels this too. We're like magnets.

"You look nice." She compliments. "Handsome. I've never seen you so dressed up."

"Don't look too bad yourself."

Her brow raises. "I have a wool coat on."

"Doesn't mean you're not beautiful in it." Her eyes light up when I say this and my heart beats out of my chest. It's been a long time since I've had a date. I'm glad the first two minutes are nowhere close to a shitshow.

On the way to the restaurant, I ask Celine if she likes her new job. She chats about her young patients and a nurse she works with named Gloria. I like the sound of Cece's voice, and it's easy to let her do most of the talking.

Royce's is set back from the road. The front end of the truck dips down into a lot below street level, lined with old oak trees. There are plenty of parking spaces, but signs direct us to the portico where a valet takes my keys. Empty-handed, I fill my palm with Cece's. Her soft fingers wrap around my burly paws. I don't have to let go when we enter the steakhouse because there's a doorman in a white jacket.

"Been here before?" I inquire as we wait to be seated.

"No. Never." She sounds excited.

A coat check girl flags Celine down and exchanges a ticket for her coat. When Cece's unwrapped, I'm conscious my jaw doesn't hit the marble floor. Her red dress fits her form and matches her shoes. It rides the slightest bit above her knee, making the tone in her trim calves mouthwatering. The same color sheer lace covers her arms and the very top. She slips the claim ticket in her purse and brushes the skirt down.

"You're perfect," I whisper from behind into her ear. Placing a hand on her hip, I slide it toward her back to guide Cece around the tables as the hostess seats us.

"This place is gigantic inside," she says with wonder after we have our menus.

"It's why I like it here. Arm room." I waggle my elbows up and down like I'm doing the chicken dance.

She tilts the menu to her face to hide her blush again before perusing the selections. I don't give Cece a chance to get self-conscious and tell her my selection is the most expensive thing. She hems and haws between two different entrees. While the sommelier opens a bottle of wine for us, I mention the seafood appetizer has a bit of everything on it. She settles on Beef Tournedos rather than surf and turf when I order apps with more than enough to share.

The waiter sets a platter of shrimp, scallops, and crab stuffed mushrooms between us. I reach for an oyster on the half shell I'd added when he took our order. Cece's eyes widen as the shellfish gets closer to my mouth.

"Have one."

"I—" She's cute stumbling over her apprehension.

I hold up a hand understanding she hasn't tried them

before. "Watch."

I set it back down on the bread plate, pretending to loosen the oyster from the liquid so she can see how it's done. "Detach." I hold up two fingers. "Slurp." The oyster slides into my mouth. "Swallow." I finish chewing, dropping the shell in an empty bowl.

"I don't want to waste them." She's holding her thumbs close to her dish, almost as if she wants to give it a go, but is afraid.

"Try one. Still plenty for me." I encourage her.

"I don't want you going hungry."

My chest heaves and I let out a wry breath. The humor is lost on Cece. She leaves me hungry all the damn time. "I don't eat much for supper." I wipe my mouth and put the napkin back in my lap, aware Cece is mimicking my exact actions to get the oyster loose. She can hate it for all I care. I've taught her something and brought her to a place she's never experienced. Whatever we've been could peter away after our meal, yet she's not forgetting tonight.

"Down the hatch?" Water dribbles off her chin. She holds the meat in her mouth, wincing before becoming brave enough to bite and swallow. "Oh, how can something so ew, taste so?"

"Good?"

"Yes, but I'm not sure I can do it again." She pushes the hors d'oeuvres plate to my side of the table. "The rest are all yours."

"Least you tried. I'm proud of you."

"Doesn't take much." She snorts.

"Lotta people wouldn't have attempted." I eat the remaining ones while Cece dips shrimp into cocktail sauce. "Graduation?" She'd promised to tell me about it.

"It was nice. Morgan and Aidy came with Carver and Sloan. We only got four tickets and I couldn't invite anyone else, which felt a little weird. So since Carver is

Carver, I wanted to express my appreciation."

"That was nice of you." I can't help wondering if she'd have included me if it was possible.

Our fingers battle for the last of the stuffed mushrooms. Mine win by default. I hold up the cap and pop it in her mouth like I've done it a million times. She holds her fingertips over her face, giggling as she chews. "You said you didn't eat a lot, but at this rate, you'll starve."

The waiter proves her wrong, setting salad bowls over our plates.

"And New Year's?" I prompt.

"My date passed out promptly at eight." She remarks of Trig and Kimber's little one, Owen, with a smile lighting up her eyes.

Is it self-deprecating to wonder if Cece's patience with kids is part of the reason it'll work between us?

While the suit puts me as much out of my element as she's out of hers, I like being here with her. In the past hour, we've relaxed into each other's company. I'm no longer worried she'll make a run for the ladies' room and climb out the window.

Chapter Nine

Celine

Dusty's saying he doesn't eat much might hold true if the bus boy hadn't removed his empty salad bowl and he wasn't still hungry. A waiter sets our entrees on the table. Everything tastes amazing, oysters included. I'm so stuffed my palm is resting on the food baby in my belly, expecting it to kick.

I'm laughing both inward and out at the charm this gruff man who puts his hands all over my body has. Despite the instances its taken for him to form a thought, Dusty has a way of engaging in conversation that makes me forget anything is amiss. Did I mention the way he fills out a suit? Or the sight of this immense man, not only knowing which fork to use, but holding itty bitty silverware? My mind has reset from grizzly bear to teddy bear

I'd thought twice while putting the finishing touches of my make-up on about what I was getting myself into. I'd picked apart the reasons behind missing a man I hardly know and considered canceling as I'd slipped on my coat. The questions got the best of me. Unsure of which answer I was more terrified of, I ran across the street to stop from chickening out. Now, there's a gnawing in my gut that I should have let Dusty pick me up.

The more we talk, the easier talking with Dusty becomes. I like how the deep timbre of his voice when it's soft and gentle has me squeezing my thighs together. It makes me feel less like whatever has happened between us *is* less because until now it's been raw. Love's not immune to sharp edges. Though, it's not as if I'm ready to fall. I have work tomorrow and my food baby is as close to any I want to carry for a long time.

I dig into my plate to be polite, already tasting the yummy leftovers they'll make reheated tomorrow. Dusty ignores that I'm eating at a snail's pace, letting me chatter at him about the past month.

"You'd think I'd have more time on my hands now. A few nights I've passed out as soon as my head has hit the pillow and others I've brought home charts to finish for the next day. The newness of it hasn't smoothed out quick enough for me to go apartment hunting. I've wanted to see a few. Holly had a lead for me too. But the places I'm interested in get gobbled up before I can call."

"Didn't know you were moving out?" he asks.

I've caught onto his speech patterns and inflection. Dusty drops I's whenever possible. The more syllables, the more likely he is to make tiny pauses since it's harder to form the word. It's becoming less noticeable and more of a quirk he has—like Northerners who add or drop an R in a word where it doesn't belong.

"I can't live at the mill forever."

"Sloan."

"Ha-ha! You're right. That's different. She humanizes Carver."

"He was plenty human before Sloan came along.

Carver doesn't want anyone the wiser."

"Still, not everyone can date a Mister Moneybags."

Dusty places both elbows on the table and leans in. "Sure about that, Cees?"

My mouth makes a little "o" and I recognize my mistake. Shit. I'm no good at this. My brother isn't the type to throw around his cash and, while we're at the classiest restaurant I've ever eaten at, I wasn't under the impression this was normal for anyone.

"I didn't mean—"

"I'm kidding, Celine. Carver's got us beat…And I'm more likely to go to Wafflehaus like you suggested."

"Why?"

"Because breakfast is the most important meal of the day…Even if you have it for dinner."

Covering my nose, I snort, and Dusty's serious expression changes to a wide grin. "I like Wafflehaus. I like greasy spoons."

"Keeping it in mind." Dusty lifts his fork as his cell phone chimes. Like a gentleman, he makes an apology to me, answering, "Hey, everything okay?" His brow furrows as he listens. He looks at his watch and then at me. "Can it wait a half an hour?" He sighs. "Okay, I'll be there as soon as I can."

"Plumbing emergency at Sweet Caroline's?" The dancers have an uncanny ability to forget the signs on the toilet stall doors and flush things they know better than to send into the old pipes.

"Six-year-old with a loose tooth."

Dusty's reply shocks me. It's funny what your brain filters out as important. Holly mentioned in passing Dusty was a father. Where I come from, those situations include a crazy ex. Since Dusty and I weren't more than fuck buddies, there's been no reason not to avoid that kind of drama. I guess it's admirable Dusty's willing to drop everything.

"Sorry about this. Soon as it's out, we can go

downtown. Get dessert to make up for the rushed meal."

"It's okay." I clutch a to-go box in my lap as we drive across town.

We arrive at a home in an older Brighton neighborhood with a big yard. It's low-slung and painted dark with chocolate trim. There are towering pine trees in the yard. The driveway has been re-paved and all the flower beds tended to. Bigger bushes have inches of pine straw mulch at the base. It's easy to come by when the trees shed their needles. There's a basket of pansies hung from the wall of a slab-style front porch so new the white variety tab sticks over the rim of the green bucket. Two white wicker chairs with faded blue patterned cushions rest underneath.

He introduces me to an older woman who opens the door before we can ring the bell and kisses her cheek. "Renata this is Cece."

She looks at the way we're dressed and gasps. "Oh gawd, Dust. When you broke your daddy/daughter night with Sylvie, I didn't know you had an actual date."

"Cece just graduated. I was taking her out to celebrate."

"College?" she asks, shaking my hand.

"PA school. I started at a medical practice recently."

"How wonderful for you. My Beth wanted to be a nurse." Renata crosses herself and looks up. I'm not sure how to respond, so it's fortunate we're interrupted.

"Daddy! I have a loose tooth!"

"Grandma said. Which one?" Dusty crouches down in front of the small girl and tucks his finger in her mouth where she's pointed. "I dunno. May take a crowbar to get out."

"Daaddddeee."

"I've got a monkey wrench in the truck. Or we could

tie a string around it, attach it to a knob, and slam the door."

"Be sewious." She places a hand on her waist, cinching in her pink princess nightgown, and juts out her hip.

"I am. This is very serious. Came as soon as I heard, so I didn't miss it."

Sylvie cocks her chin, looking over her father's shoulder. "Who are you?"

"Celine Wescott." I dip down, mimicking Dusty's posture, to hold out my hand.

"Sylvie Rhys Alston."

"Sylvie—"

"Sylvie Rhys Yates," she mutters, giving me a last name that's not the same as Dusty's. Her lips pinch like she's sucked a lemon, but her attitude changes on a dime. "I have a loose tooth!" She pokes toward her mouth. It's the first time I notice a hairline silver scar running to her columella, where the septal cartilage for her nose is.

"How exciting!" I gush the same way when my patients tell me something important.

"You're pretty." She touches the lace on my dress.

"Thank you." I turn the same color as the fabric. "So are you."

My heart is melting. Sylvie has fine honeyed-chestnut hair and huge blue eyes. From the sassy way she interacts with her dad to how outgoing and polite she is meeting someone new, everything about her is adorable.

"So...what're we doing about the tooth?" Dusty prompts.

"Nothing. I wanted you to see," she states, matter of fact.

I rise from the carpet. A nagging sensation overtakes my quads. If I don't start working out again soon, being out of shape will make it harder to keep my balance.

"Sylvie's been wiggling it so much, it's a wonder it didn't fall out before you got here." Renata supplies.

She's standing near a couch that's a lot newer than the cushions outside. The living room is a mix of old and new. Thin gold-framed school pictures dot the walls. The aging girl in them looks a lot like Sylvie. On a side table is a family snapshot of Dusty and the woman from the pictures. She holds a baby with pigtails in her lap. While Renata's been nothing less than welcoming, I feel like I'm intruding on something sacred.

"Give you a buck if you pull it." Dusty offers.

"What if the Tooth Fairy doesn't come?" Sylvie's lower lip trembles.

"Because I paid you?

She nods slowly. Her big blue eyes widen with fear.

Dusty bats a hand at her. "Down payment. It might impress the Tooth Fairy. She may be short on teeth."

"The Tooth Fairy might run out of teeth?" Sylvie becomes concerned.

"Your choice, Peanut." Dusty looks again at his watch and me. This time his expression is different. Almost as if he's torn between wanting to be in two places at once. He doesn't want to miss this. The level of sweetness is enough to make your tooth ache. "I can't stick around long. Miss Celine needs a ride home."

I'm not sure who has a bigger frown, Sylvie or me. I hadn't realized the night was ending so soon.

"Will you help me?"

"Sure, but no crying."

Dusty hefts his daughter up, pretending to let out a groan about how big the light-as-a-feather tyke is getting and brings her to the bathroom. I hear wood scraping across the linoleum and Dusty tells her to get up on a stool so she can look in the mirror afterward.

Renata comes to stand by my side. "She's a tough

cookie, but I'll warn you Sylvie will turn on the waterworks when he tucks her into bed. She and Dusty are real close. Don't you worry or feel bad, though her daddy's smart enough to know she's putting on a show. He's strict with my granddaughter, but lays the world at her feet, that man."

"DID YOU GET IT!" I hear Sylvie shout a moment later.

"I got it."

"It's *small*." She sounds disappointed.

"Nah, it's the right size for what the Tooth Fairy needs."

The wood scrapes across the floor again and they emerge into the hallway. Sylvie is over Dusty's shoulder superhero-style with her arms stretched wide. She pulls them in so they can enter the room across the hall, and I notice she's clutching a green bill in her hand.

"The Tooth Fairy will still come?" Questions a small voice.

Renata and I keep eavesdropping. Sylvie's grandma is incredibly hospitable, but the cuteness overload between daddy and daughter is what eases the discomfort of not knowing what to say to Renata. It must be odd for me to be here as Dusty's date and not her daughter, Beth. It's bizarre enough for me since I knew nothing about Dusty's personal life until tonight.

Dusty and Sylvie's voices have fallen to a murmur in her bedroom.

"Don't goooooo!" She wails as I see Dusty fill the threshold.

"Cue the cryin'." Renata laughs.

Dusty reminds Sylvie I need to go home. Heaviness settles in the pit of my stomach. I'm the reason she's upset her dad is leaving.

"I want to say goodbye," Sylvie huffs. I imagine her arms crossing over the princess nightie.

"If your Daddy says 'yes' are you going to cut the

crocodile tears?" Still standing next to me, Renata puts her foot down.

Sylvie must've agreed since Dusty motions for me.

"Goodnight," I say, popping my head into the room.

"Bye. It was nice to meet you."

"It was very nice to meet you too, Sylvie Rhys." This gets me a front-row seat for her wide grin missing the top tooth.

Dusty ushers me out after telling Sylvie how much he loves her. He expects she'll be sleeping when he gets home. There won't be anything under her pillow tomorrow otherwise, and he doesn't want her disappointed. Renata switches places with him, waving us off so we'll go before Sylvie is the wiser.

Chapter Ten

"Thanks." I appreciate Cece being a good sport. Doubtless, many women are thrilled to have a date interrupted by a kindergartner and Cece hesitated to accept my invitation to begin with.

"It wasn't a big deal. She's sweet. Like her dad." I catch her smile in the streetlight as we enter the dessert bar. "Must run in the family."

A member of the waitstaff seats us at a small cafe table and we both order hot liqueured drinks as they list the specialties. It's a cramped venue and the way the table's situated, we're surrounded. Cees is so close we're practically in each other's lap. When the barista leaves to get our desserts, I'm cautious of my elbows and moving too fast so I don't inadvertently elbow a server with a tray full of drinks.

"Sylvie's not mine," I confide. "Knew I loved her before she was born, though. Beth's husband, Ben, was stationed at Fort Bragg down in Fayetteville. He died in Iraq while she was pregnant. Beth was a friend. We started dating months afterward. Beth was farther along in her pregnancy. Best day of my life being there when Sylvie took her first breath. Until losing Beth, the worst moments were being helpless when people looked sideways at Sylvie."

Cece hardly flinches. The compassion as she says, "Meaning her cleft lip" is as conversational as me responding, "You noticed her scar." It doesn't phase her in the least.

I've spent a lifetime learning to compartmentalize the way others view me. First, it was my size. Now it's my speech. But defending someone you love, especially when it's your kid, is a different ballgame. You wanna build them up so they're strong enough to deal with those emotions. You want to turn the other cheek and say it doesn't get under your skin. But most of all, you want to throat-punch anyone who looks at them sideways.

"Beth cr-reated her with someone else, but I've always considered Sylvie my child. When she came roaring into the world, I'd already decided to protect my daughter." I was there when the nurses wheeled her into all of her surgeries and on bended knee until she was out of recovery. "It made Beth's death worse. We were never married. I have no rights to our beautiful little girl."

"How did Beth die?" She hesitates to ask. Cece seems as fearful of my answer as I am to recount it in such a public place. Yet, the tinkling of dessert forks, glasses, and the loud crowd surrounding us add a layer of anonymity. I can get through telling her, and if my eyes water, then it's not in front of anyone who knows me besides Cece.

I scrub a hand over my lower jaw. "We were on I-40 coming back from a concert. Teens were tossing rocks from the overpass. Experimenting to see if they bounce off of windshields... Newsflash: they don't. A ten-pound shattered the glass. Hit Beth in the chest. I lost control of the car and we hit a cement pylon."

"Oh, Dusty, How awful! I'm so sorry for your loss."

"Thanks." What else do you say to the sentiment? I explain to Celine my biggest regret is not marrying Beth when I had the chance, so my daughter doesn't have to live with her grandmother.

"Renata won't sign over guardianship?"

"She would. Ben's mom is still alive. He was Mrs. Yates's only child. Sylvie is her last connection to him." Sylvie's too young to have already lost this much. I won't drag it through the courts to get my way. "Ben's mother is battling stage four cancer. Our time will come. Besides, I'm still the one tucking Sylvie in most nights."

"Renata said you missed your daddy/daughter date tonight. Was that for me?"

"I'll make it up to her," I say in the same reassuring tone I used with Sylvie.

The waitstaff is back with a piece of triple chocolate layer cake for Cece and a raspberry mousse tart with dark chocolate crust for me.

"You dropped everything when Sylvie needed you. It says a lot for your character."

"Yeah, whipped by a member of the Cartoon Princess Mafia." I lift a spoon of Chambord cream to her lips, nudging Celine to open up.

Cece laughs, "You'll appreciate it someday. So will she," before accepting the bite. "Wow! That was tastier than I thought."

"So what about your family?" Settling back in the too small for my stature chair, I try blending in with my surroundings. I have the same awkward sense I do when Sylvie makes me play tea party.

"My parents fed and clothed us until we were eighteen and sent us on our way. They struggled for what they had and what they could give us. Then Morgan got in trouble and any lingering closeness we had disappeared overnight. Guilt-by-association was an embarrassment for my father in a rural town... My mother still gets in touch, on occasion. I kept my dancing at Sweet Caroline's from them because I was afraid of how they'd react. Now, with it in the past, it's none of their business how I afforded my degree and who helped me get where I am today when they refused. Sometimes the family you wind up with is the one you find along the way, right?"

I nod, understanding. "You've still got your brother."

"Which makes our relationship all the more special. I have some regrets. I mean, I was the one who asked Carver to find Morgan a job when he was released from prison."

"That doesn't make him a bad man. Morgan's my friend. His jail time doesn't change anything." I may get sick of Morgan's overprotectiveness, but I can't blame him. I comprehend the why of wanting to keep your family out of harm's way and doubt if Skye made a play for Celine he'd act any differently. "Neither does how any of us rake in extra cash."

I stop, letting the last line soak in for Cece. I'm paid well doing maintenance at the factory and strip club. Skye invests a portion of my salary. I don't ask in what. All I know is he hands me a paper once a quarter showing how much it's grown by. Even with a professional income, I never believed I'd see that kind of money. It's enough to cover any concerns over what might happen to Sylvie if I weren't around. Renata will have enough to raise her and then some. I've offered to get us a newer, bigger place to live, but Renata is content in the home she made for her family. Anytime something needs replacing, I take care of it because she's taking care of us.

Celine looks as if a cat's got her tongue before she gets the gumption to ask, "How'd you get roped into working at the mill?"

"Carver and I grew up in the same trailer park... Well, for a time we did. Both my parents were out of work... He's always been the sort who you think doesn't notice you and is out for themselves. But he looks out for the little guy."

"You're hardly a little guy, Dusty." She teases, squeezing my bicep. The jolt goes straight to my dick and I'm glad the table cloth is hiding my lap. Any man can walk around semi-hard at Sweet Caroline's and no one gives a crap if you're horny or not. A classy place like this is another story. Damn, my fingers ache to touch Cees. To feel the zap of electricity between us. And I know she likes it when I do.

"Renata knows about your job?" she pries.

"She knows my handyman salary is invested if that's what you mean. Got a decent chunk from the legal settlement. So did she as Beth's mother. I don't do more than fix broken stuff if it's also what you're asking."

"What about your parents?"

"North Carolina got too cold for them. They're in Florida."

"That makes so much sense to me. I'm not the biggest fan of winter. So what did you do before the accident?" A ghost of a grimace appears on her face as if she doesn't want to dredge up more awful memories.

Reaching across the table, I cover her small hand with my larger one. "I was an electrical engineer. I liked tinkering when I was a kid, taking things apart to see how it worked. Using spare parts of broken stuff—alarm clocks, radios, handheld video games—and fixing it."

"You didn't want to go back to it?"

"My recovery took a year. Still get headaches. I try to keep them at a minimum. It's difficult to work a normal job. Plus, hiring managers have a hard time with my sluggish speech. Combined with the way I look? Their first instinct is there's not much going on in between my ears." The bigger the sentence, the longer it takes to get everything out of my head. I tap my temple reassuring her it's all up there.

"That's not fair."

I give Cece a knowing look. She darts her gaze away. I'm not stupid as to what she's thought of me. Sometimes you see what's on the outside of a person before you get a glimpse of the inside. The fact that our first encounters were one-sided—with Cece taking off her clothes in front of a crowd while I watched—isn't lost on me. My initial attraction to her was shallow.

I tip up her chin so her pretty dark brown eyes connect with mine. I'm not ashamed of the way we started out, and I don't want her to be either. What I want is for us to move on to the next phase.

"Doing what I do gives me plenty of time with my kid. That's the most important thing. To me."

"I understand," she says.

It seems like we have mutual respect for the way one another leads their life. If she'd been mine, I'd have been more overbearing. My jealousy aside, Cees has proven she has a one-track mind to achieve her goals. I was never upset at her, but the way other men ogled her.

The table gets cleared and as we're waiting on the check, Cece lets my thumb graze over her knuckles in soft swirls. This is definitely how I'd imagined it would go and how I see taking her out again. The naturalness of being in public is freeing and the best part of getting to know Cece better someplace where we have no explaining to do. It's our choice whether we decide to tell people this is a continuation of a long-standing attraction we've kept quiet or the start of something entirely new. I'm one step closer to being able to show our friends how I feel about this woman.

Chapter Eleven

Celine

Dusty uses the back alley behind the factory to pull into the parking lot. He maneuvers the truck into a spot away from the harsh street lights and kills the engine.

"Hope you had a nice time tonight." He rubs the back of his neck. "Haven't taken anyone out in a while. I'm rusty."

"I had a wonderful time. Sylvie is great. I bet you can't wait to get home to her."

"She'll be fast asleep."

"I hope the Tooth Fairy comes before she wakes." I have a plastic baggie tucked in a box, filled with my baby teeth. When I was small, I kept them in case it was a magical mishap that she'd forgotten to visit our house.

His chin tips down and his lips spread into a sheepish smile, showing a genuine amount of pearly whites and proving he's smitten by his daughter.

"Well, ah, goodnight. Thank you." I'm the first to lean in, planning to give Dusty the briefest kiss farewell.

Our lips brush against one another's and his beefy palm encases the side of my head. I've tried to stick to casual-acquaintances-bordering-on-friends. The reality is, until this evening, the carnal knowledge Dusty and I shared was all we knew of each other. I haven't led him on. Yet, I'm back to the night he walked me across the street from my shift at Sweet Caroline's. When I tried to flirt and he took the opportunity with his lips, igniting sparks.

Dusty deepens the kiss, our tongues taste the lingering sweetness from our desserts. He grips my hip, sliding me closer. The same hand that cupped my face with such tenderness slides under the hem of my dress. The skirt has inched above my waist. His fingers dig into my skin, searching for something that's not there. They skid to a stop, almost like the scratch of a needle against a record.

"Shit. Where are your panties?"

"I don't wear them. I don't like them." I developed the bad habit after I started dancing. It was one thing enduring the bottom half of my costume riding up my ass for an hour, but the way the g-strings cinched against my hips? The way it aggravated my senses led to any style of underwear doing the same. I have a handful in my lingerie drawer for modesty's sake when there is no choice than to put them on.

"You've been bare-ass naked, sitting across the table from me, and never said a word." Dusty's possessive growl is enough to make me cream my panties. If I had any on.

"The top of me is covered," I tease.

"Not for fucking long."

His fingers skim the insides of my thighs. Nudging up, he flicks a knuckle against my sensitive areas. For the first time, I understand why Dusty excels at his job and how his engineering background gave him the boost to tackle so many tasks. Before he's reached back to unbutton the top of my dress I'm done for. He might not realize he's doing two things at once, but the multiple things he is doing have every part of me anticipating what's next.

I reach for his belt, unbuckling it, and loosening the fly on his dress pants. With his fingers plunging inside of me, Dusty doesn't miss a beat. He shimmies his hips up. I spring his thick cock from his boxer briefs.

"This would be a lot easier if you went commando too," I suggest, nipping at his lips.

"Taking it under advisement."

In a smooth motion, he grabs me by the waist, hauling me over his lap to straddle his hips. I sit down on his impossibly hard length, moaning as he stretches me deep.

"Oh God, you're huge." I'd forgotten how well-endowed Dusty is.

"Appreciate the compliment."

I laugh. The dirty words Dusty whispers in my ear aside, we never say anything to one another when we're screwing. This is the first time we're not forced into silence and the conversation strikes me as humorous. Dusty catches the soft, feminine giggle with a mischievous bite to my lower lip. His hands move back to my shoulders, tugging down the top of my dress. The fabric pools at my midsection.

"Christ, no bra either?"

I won't answer. I normally wear one of those. This bodice has built-in cups. His hands are now doing a fantastic job of keeping the tits that have provided me an income pinned to my chest. This isn't the moment to inspect how the garment's sewn together when I'm about to fall apart.

He sucks on my neck, a nipple, my arms, any place my skin can meet his mouth.

"Fuck me harder, Cees." Dusty commands.

With each rise and fall on my knees, he thrusts up,

grinding the base of his cock against my clit. I'm so full when he's inside of me, I think there isn't any more I can take. Yet, when I slide up, my body yearns for that fullness and I want more.

In the darkness, I see the strain in his expression as he holds off, waiting to chase my orgasm with his. Never once has Dusty come before I have.

I want his consideration as a lover to be enough. But I let go for the first time, my voice unrestrained, reliving all the other moments I've let him hold dominion over me. Use my body. Be to Dusty what all the men who sit in the audience watching me strip want me to be for them.

Familiar warmth pulses inside of me. I slide against his broad chest. The beginning was good. The end was better. I wish that somewhere in between my past as an exotic dancer hadn't crept in and my subconscious hadn't labeled me a slut for sleeping with a man on a first date.

Our fiery breaths have fogged the windows, making something about the cabin claustrophobic. I adjust my top and zip up. Dusty uses fast food napkins from the glove box to wipe between my thighs. Disposing of them on the floorboard by my red shoes.

He brushes his knuckles against my cheek. I shift away as if a bee has stung me instead of reveling in the electricity of his touch the way I had before. Placing a swift kiss at the corner of his lips, in a hurry I thank him again for a wonderful night. Sitting up straight so he can't chase me down again like the second swallow after a cheap shot of whiskey, I slide off of the seat and my toes hit the pavement.

"Hey." He grabs my wrist as "When can I see you again?"

Again?

The shock on my face must be a dead giveaway. Dusty's expression blanks and he lets go of my arm.

I enjoyed his company. Dusty behaved like a perfect gentleman until neither of us wanted him to be. Then we were right back to who we've always been to one another. I can't say I expected the night to end any other way. However, mentally back to being the whore whose John pays with an expensive steak and an even more costly bottle of wine, I hadn't allowed myself to consider he'd ask me out again.

"I'll see you around the mill before moving out, won't I?" I'm evasive. Doubtless, we'll run into one another *after* I've had time to process tonight.

The overhead dome light is on. Dusty's dark eyes bore into me. It's not what he meant. My gut tells me I've blown it with the nicest guy I'll ever meet.

"I'm busy with work." I make a foolish excuse.

He nods. "Thanks for coming out tonight, Cees. Happy graduation."

I lower my gaze to the gravel, closing the door. My high-heels *clip-clop* over the parking lot.

I've hardly gone a few yards when the truck engine roars to life and the headlights illuminate the path to the building's well-lit back entrance. It shifts into drive, but the screech of the brakes has me turning to look back as it shudders to a stop.

Dusty gets out of the truck and rounds the hood. His right fist pounds twice on the metal and his left palm reaches out to encircle my waist. He draws me to his chest before his fist tangles in my hair, bringing me in closer for a toe-curling kiss.

I stumble in my heels, touching my lips. "What was that for?"

"Bye, Cees." He's walking backward as it dawns on me Dusty means it. We've never said goodbye. It's so… final. My heart and my jaw are scraping the pavement with the sting of a skinned knee.

"But—"

"But what?" His spine stiffens to the point I swear I

hear it crack. "What are we doing here?" His arms stretch wide in question. "Why bother to come out if it wasn't to let me down easy?"

"What do you want from me?"

"A fucking chance?" He musses his hair. "God, I've never met a woman more interested in a quick roll and less intent on a second date than you." He bats a hand as if I'm not worth his time.

"Why?"

"Cause you're gorgeous. And smart. And *I* liked hanging out with you as much as I like banging you, Celine."

The emphasis in those last words is caustic, cutting me for being the user, for acting like I'm entitled to use Dusty's body and not care about his feelings. I hang my head, understanding I'm more than playing hard to get. I'm the player in this scenario, and I'm treating Dusty unfairly.

Dusty's hands are in his pockets. He's rolled his shirtsleeves to his elbows. The jovial smile he wore all night has vanished and I'm left with a cold dead stare.

I miss the guy he introduced me to this evening, the way I'd missed the man who'd cover my body with his over the past month.

"Where would we go?" I ask, wondering if my question is about a physical location or if I'm speaking to myself, curious over how we could ever make a go of a relationship. I'm not in the best headspace for it and can't explain why.

He shrugs as if he doesn't care. "Headed to Boone Friday night. You can come." His thumb covers his mouth. He's second-guessing if asking me to go away for the weekend was wrong. "You're busy. I get it." He's not even looking at me anymore.

My mouth's agape. All of a sudden, this train is moving too fast, but if I don't start running in the same direction now, I'll never keep up. "Can I bring my charts to catch up on?"

"Yeah… uh… You like to hike? ski?"

"I haven't been in a long time. Hike, that is." I've never skied.

"It's cold, so pack a winter jacket. Extra socks."

"Maybe some long underwear."

"Some plain 'ol underwear too." He smirks and I almost see the man he'd acted like at dinner. "Stop your butt from getting cold while we walk."

I laugh when he jokes at my expense. I deserve it.

"Are you sure about this, Cees?"

"I'm still trying to figure out what we're do—" I pause. "Why me?" *Why him and why now?*

"Told you. Want a chance to see where it goes."

"I guess it's going to Boone."

Chapter Twelve

Celine

Daybreak is an hour away when I slide a pair of tailored pants over my hips and tuck the fitted blouse into the waist. My new wardrobe selection beats what I used to wear to work. Not only am I covered from neck to ankles, the lines of the fabric contour my curves instead of highlighting where my body flares to ignite a man's fire.

"Knock, knock. I brought you some elixir of the gods."

I kick my new red dress under the bed frame as Sloan slips through the doorway to my room.

"Thanks. So what's up?" I take the hot mug.

"Why does anything have to be up?"

"The one person who lives and dies by caffeine is Kimber. She's your go-to when things are shaky. I know when I'm being used as a poor substitute."

The three of us have hung together the longest—since before Trig and Kimber got married. But where I'm a generation younger, the connection between Sloan and Kimber runs deeper.

"Nothing is wrong between me and Carver." She pinches her forehead like she has a headache.

"If you say so," I reply with a noncommittal shrug.

It's only six am. The bags under Sloan's eyes are a dead giveaway that she's had a long night. And not in the same way my late arrival home was.

Sloan's butt is about to hit my mattress when she jumps up like something bit her. "What is that?"

"Huh?" I glance behind me, pushing the top button through the buttonhole of my shirt.

"You have a hickey!" She points to the broken blood vessels to the side above where my cleavage starts. "You got some! When did you get some?"

"I did not." I slap her hand away as she tugs at my collar, trying to inspect the handyman's handiwork.

"You did. Your face is almost as red as the bruise. Strike one for celibacy! You'll be open for business soon. If you're not already. Who knew the sexy librarian look was as much of a turn on as they say? Hell, how long was he clamped on to you? That's some suction." Her brows waggle.

"Do not go there."

But she does anyway. "Whoever it was and whatever else they did, you loved it or else you wouldn't be sporting a lip tattoo."

"He did not! I am not open for anything!" I can't admit to Sloan I haven't been abstaining or living off of the self-love glove. There hasn't been a reason to touch myself other than pretending it got me amped up while I stripped. Dusty's taken care of my every need.

I run a brush through my hair, twist, and pile it up on top of my head, securing it with a clip.

"You're not spilling even a tiny detail? You didn't even mention you had a date—or did you swipe right and it was a hook-up?—Please, you've got to give me a crumb!" From the other side of the bed, she helps me drag the comforter up and fluff the pillows.

"You're so domestic," I tease, trying to distract her. Sloan shares a full-fledged apartment with Carver on the other side of the building. The top two floors here are also part of the household to do with as she deems fit.

She flashes me a smarmy face and flops on the pillow, messing up the neatness, and unwilling to give up. "So?"

I'm not sure where to start the explanation. Dusty hadn't told me not to tell anyone we'd gone out. Yet, this is new and I'm still curious whether this becomes anything more.

Also, the reason I ran across the street to meet him in Sweet Caroline's parking lot wasn't as innocuous as I'd let on. I'd been so anxious previous to our date that I'd blow it. I worried I wouldn't be as strong as Holly seems if our friends teased me, and whether or not they'd understand I found more about Dusty attractive than his rugged appearance. I didn't want to get defensive, answering snide comments. Or trapped when one of the girls taunted me about his size when we all would know they meant his *size*. I'm not ready for the questions because I'm not sure why this is happening now and with him.

I spent the night tossing and turning in bed. I'm unable to let go of the course I've drafted for a man, no matter how sexy he is or how amazing the orgasms are with him. Sloan has her Mister Right. Mine's not supposed to show up right now. It's too soon.

"We went to dinner. I had a nice time. He was a gentleman. I met his daughter. We went to dessert."

"Whoa! Back up. He introduced you to his kid? Men don't do that. They hide children until you're hooked and then spring them on you."

"Are you speaking from experience?" She doesn't mean Carver. He has no kids.

"Damn straight." Sloan pauses. "Cece, he's serious.

He's not hiding. This guy may really like you."

I try ignoring the fact Sylvie was sort of sprung on me. However, it wasn't as if I'd asked Dusty for details about his life before last night. We were fuck-buddies. All I had to know to make him happy was how to jerk him off. I'm also not ready for kids. Mine or anyone else's.

"Ooorr he's trying to scare me off." I'm hopeful this will make Sloan drop the subject.

"You're a pediatric physician's assistant. Kids puke on you. It'll take more than a child's existence for that to happen."

I loop a hoop into my earlobe and sip the last of my java juice.

"At least tell me if you're seeing him again."

"I am."

She squeals.

"Okay, now that my silly life has distracted you, wanna tell me what's going on?" I sit next to Sloan and take her hand. "Kimber won't be up for hours and you seem like you need an ear."

"Carver wants to go on vacation."

"How's it an issue?" The two of them are always jetting off somewhere for business, which I never pry about.

"This is a make life-changing decisions kind of trip."

"So all play and no work? Sloan, you could have worse problems than lying on a beach having your rich, hot man cater to your every toe-curling need."

"I'm not ready."

"And I'm not ready for a relationship at all, but here we both are. Two peas in a pod!" I sing out, tapping her knee and standing.

When it comes down to it being someone's girlfriend, let alone wife is too far out of my scope of reality. But a tiny piece of me doesn't want to lose Dusty and that part is in my chest, not my hooha. It's why I've decided to say fuck it and go to Boone. Yet, I'm still not sure how after this weekend Dusty and I can keep dating casual.

And how do I explain to Sloan he's not the man he seems? Sure, she has an open mind, but Dusty is big and he does talk with a stutter. Am I going to get defensive of him to my friends? If they found out we've been having sex all these months, will they think I'm taking advantage? Some of these things I've hypothesized over before. But Kimber and Sloan also have men of means, and I hadn't considered anyone would claim I was a gold digger until last night while trying to fall asleep. It adds to the list of reasons I'm screwed if anyone finds out and whatever this is falls apart.

I gather my stuff for work and we head toward the kitchen so I can toast a plain bagel to eat on my drive in. Bumping down the hall, I ask Sloan if she wants to look at apartments with me.

"The other thing I'm not ready for is you moving out."

"Aw, Hailey's still here." Sloan's brother, Jasper, and his much younger girlfriend share a room on the floor below. Hailey all but grew up at the mill.

"If I'd done what was right, she'd have spread her wings and be gone. Maybe I was afraid I'd miss her too much."

"I want to say I'll stay put for your sake, Sloan. But I've had two goals; graduating and getting my own place. Carver's done so much for me already. It's not fair to take advantage." Especially when I've been breaking his rules.

"Kimber did—"

"And Kimber left when she got pregnant and married Trig. She comes back to visit. So will I. All my besties hang here. How about we make a deal. I stay until you've helped me find the perfect situation." Sloan's about to pounce on my offer. "But you can't KO every apartment for a stupid reason. It's gotta be legit."

"Fine," she deadpans. We walk across the old wooden floors and by the couches, pushing the swinging kitchen doors open. "I'll even help you this weekend."

"I've sort of got plans."

"With suction man?" Sloan ribs me.

I don't answer, but shove her and we share a laugh at my expense.

The factory kitchen is strictly utilitarian, but gorgeous nonetheless. The cupboards are gray with white marble countertops. An exposed brick wall with copper piping attached holds long wooden shelves. Bowls, plates, and platters—stacked by the dozen—rest on the lower row and there are baking dishes on the higher ones. Underneath are drawers for flatware, cups, and juice glasses. The opposite side has commercial refrigerators and freezers facing a row of dishwashers underneath the granite. On the far wall are the ranges with insane amounts of burners and so many regular and warming ovens it's impossible to keep straight which door does what. A huge window over a six-foot sink floods the kitchen with natural light. There's a pantry at the end.

I place my coffee mug in the sink and soap it up before rinsing it with an industrial faucet sprayer. Then I dry and place it on a cup hook underneath the shelving. Sloan rolls her eyes at me for not tossing it in the dishwasher. It's a single dirty dish, and this was my designated chore growing up.

Sticking my tongue out at her, I reach for the tray of goodies delivered mid-week from the shop where Aidy works. I slice and toast a bagel. While it's cooking, I snag a paper sack and the last chocolate croissant for Gloria. She loved the fresh one I'd brought her from the store on Monday.

As the toaster pops, Carver bangs through the doors in a grumpy mood. The scowl on his unshaved face proves he woke up on the wrong side of the bed. He barks at Sloan, reminding me they've had a tough night. He's also barefoot in a robe with wet hair. Suds drip off his earlobe.

"Our hot water is out. Why did I buy this place? It's a money pit."

"It is not." Sloan turns the kitchen tap and splashes her fingers through it. "This one is fine. Must be a problem with the apartment's water heater. I'll text Dusty to see when he can come check it out."

Carver exits in a huff the likes I've never seen, muttering about what he's supposed to do in the meantime.

"Rinse your damn head, Mister I'm-supposed-to-know-everything." She faces me as the door to their apartment bangs shut.

His stomps up the staircase to their room are audible through the wall. He's definitely in a snit over their argument. Carver hasn't treated Sloan this way since she got here. Back then, the two weren't on the best of terms. And for all of the silly nicknames she gives him, Sloan hasn't sneered, shooting double-fisted middle fingers, in the wake of Carver's demands the way she is right now in longer than I can recall.

"Are you laughing?" Sloan pulls her cell from her pocket.

"Huh?" I touch my face. I'd felt the strange tugging as the corners of my lips turned up when they mentioned the handyman. "No. I'm sorry y'all aren't getting along." I apologize and take my cue to leave.

Chapter Thirteen

Dusty

I'm packing what little I don't keep a spare of up in Boone into my toiletry kit when Renata pushes her shoulder against the hall bathroom's door jamb.

"So can I ask?" She crosses her arms, smirking.

Next to Holly, Renata's the one woman I'm closest with. She's as adept at teasing as giving sound advice. Although, I have to admit I'd prefer asking Holly for help with my women problems since it's strange to have Beth's mom tell me what to do now. Funny enough, whenever Beth and I had disagreements, Renata was right there lending me an ear.

I look at her and nod, not quite agreeing but Renata's not nosy for no reason. She keeps me protected like a fledgling under her wing, no different than the way she treats my daughter.

"I'm taking her."

"And her *is*?"

"Don't be coy, Renata." I point a bottle of aftershave in her direction, then plop it in the kit.

"I want to hear it come out of your mouth. You

wouldn't bring cologne and extra mouthwash if you were going to the mountains with Holly."

"Fine, I'm spending the weekend with Celine." My tone is gruff and my spine rankles.

"That's nice. That's *very* nice, Dust." Renata's got a shit-eating grin on her face. "Celine is an attractive girl, and she works for a doctor." I take her compliments as a seal of approval until she says, "Don't rush it."

She's already waltzing to the kitchen and I chase Renata down the hall. "What do you mean?"

Renata twirls and places her hand on the back of a stool. "You have a little girl."

I swing my hand in the air, encouraging her to get on with whatever she needs to say. I don't get the impression Renata doesn't like Cece. The vibe is more a warning I'll blow it if I'm not careful.

"I'm not talking down about my daughter by telling you that you didn't look at my Beth the way you do her. I told you Celine is beautiful, but what you see in her, Dusty. You need to ask yourself, does it go further than desire? Because starting something significant with Celine includes Sylvie. You'll have to make room in your schedule for both of them."

"And you suppose Celine's going to take up more of my time. Sylvie's time."

"It could. How are you planning to juggle both? Are you even sure Celine is interested in dating a man with a child?"

I ignore Renata's insinuation. I can be there for both of them. Cece didn't have a problem with our date's interruption. This is manageable. Single dads have relationships.

"What I'm not very tactfully putting out there is; one date and you're off on a weekend getaway?"

I rub the heels of my palms into my eye sockets, unwilling to correct her. I'm not about to explain the timeframe of my connection with Celine to Renata. Her best intentions aside, I can't get into my sex life with my daughter's grandmother.

"Be careful is all I'm saying, and badly given your reaction. You and she may want different things outta life. Your time with Beth got cut short and Celine's not simply a continuation of where you were the day before the accident just with somebody new. She's gotta catch up."

"I know." I grit out, tired of listening to Renata the way I'd been as a teenager with my own parents.

If she had the whole story, I'm certain Renata might sing a different tune. Cece and I have a chance now that everything can be out in the open. It's one we're taking this weekend.

"Don't be so led by your heart taking her away that you can't make choices with the brain God gave you." She scolds me with a wink and a smile. "Now scoot. If you're still home when I get back from picking Sylvie up in the carpool line, she'll convince you to bring her. I doubt Celine agreed to a kid tagging along on a romantic getaway."

I'm about to argue with Renata that it's not lovey-dovey when she tugs me into a hug. "Be safe. Driving. With your heart, and hers. I love ya."

I take her advice—the part about making myself scarce before Sylvie gets home from school anyway—and head to fill my vehicle up before driving over to the medical complex to pick up Cece.

The pediatric office closes early every other Friday afternoon. She's opted to stay late to finish some charts. I shoot off a text after parking and meet her at the rear of her car, which is in almost the same spot as it was last week. Cece's got a thick parka folded in her arms, her purse slung over one shoulder, and laptop bag counterbalancing on the other.

"I hope you don't mind I brought work. I only have a few left to catch up on for Monday." She pops the trunk and I don't give her the opportunity to add her overnight bag to the weight she's carrying.

I shake my head, closing the lid. "Not worried. Have plenty on my fix-it list while you're busy."

Her brow furrows.

"The place we're headed is mine. Sylvie comes with about once a month to give Renata a break from us."

"And Renata's okay with keeping her this weekend while you're gone?"

It takes me a minute to explain the other times Renata comes too. "She's leaving on a cruise with friends. She travels fr-requently. When that happens she sends me up there first, on my own, for some peace and quiet."

"You've got this parenting gig figured out." Cece slides into the truck.

I put her bag in the back and she hands her computer and coat over the seat, keeping her purse at her feet.

"We appreciate one another. Renata was all done raising children. She stepped up for Sylvie's sake."

"Same as you did."

"In some respects, yes." I love my daughter with my whole heart and only want the best people surrounding her.

Some might argue what goes on at the mill disqualifies the men I work for. But they have an unwritten pact to stand up for one another. I've watched the kindness extend to the little guy, or gal in Celine's case. Carver plays using his own rule book, but who doesn't nowadays?

"Need anything before we hit the road?" I ask. It's about a three-hour drive. I'll make a pit stop two-thirds of the way there since my kindergartner has trained my bladder to react like Pavlov's dogs when I see the rest area stop sign.

"Nope," she replies as I turn the key. "Dusty?"

Cees licks her full lips and I don't give her a chance

to change her mind. I cup her cheek and our lips connect. The kiss is slower, steadier than what we're used to, and much too short. I can only stop because I know what's waiting for us once the Appalachians are on the horizon.

"I'm glad we're doing this."

"Me too." I finger the interlacing plaits of the braid dangling over her chest.

Cece's more casual today. Jeans and a white blouse with a gray sweater have turned her into a cross between the girl I've watched at the factory for years and the professional I met coming out of the building last week.

As we hit the highway, she slips off her shoes and puts her feet up on the dash.

"Your toenail polish matches your necklace," I comment as she stretches out. It's a bright summery teal and her pounded metal jewelry has a turquoise inset.

She makes a move to put her toes back into her shoes.

"No." I stop her by lacing our fingers together and kissing the back of her hand. I'm glad she's comfortable enough to do this.

She gives me a shy smile. "I should've asked first."

"It's no problem." Between me and Sylvie, the interior had been a sticky mess with wrappers and cracker crumbs wedged in the crevices. I've been more meticulous about my habits since having it detailed.

Celine insists she's monopolizing the conversation. I tune the radio to fill the awkward gaps and notice we both mouth the words to the same country songs.

If she wasn't here, I'd belt them out. Lyrics are second nature. Synapses easily reroute signals forming the next sound, and my brain and tongue work in coordination without delay. The practice helps, and this was one of the therapies I was best at. The one I keep up with because it requires scant effort and I enjoy it. Life doesn't have to be hard if you don't want it to be.

A half an hour before the rest stop, Cees gets quiet. She's watching the green signs pass on the right, her neck almost craning as we speed by. Her hands wring in her lap, and I'm worried she's about to take a chunk out of her lower lip. It keeps disappearing and the cute lip bite thing she does is more akin to a shark mauling its prey.

"You good?" There's a lump in my throat.

We're fairly far west of Winston-Salem, but I'll take the nearest offramp and swing back east if Cece has changed her mind. I don't want her to feel trapped all weekend.

The next destination marker is in view when she speaks. "I lived there. It's where we grew up." She shivers, pulling the edges of her sweater closer together.

I make a muffled sound acknowledging so she'll go on, and crank up the heat in the cab. But Cece frowns, staring down at her hands as if she's only noticed the frantic and rhythmic motion her thumbs are making. To stop herself, she tugs off the band securing her braid, combing her fingers through it and her hair falls in loose kinky waves down her neck.

A mile later we pass the exit sign. Even in winter, the thick foliage is overgrown and, with the sun setting, the dingy white letters of the town name are hard to make out. My guess is this far in the sticks it's no more than a map dot on the road to nowhere. However, with Cece being so silent, I'm conscious of keeping negative thoughts about her childhood home to myself. It's not as if the towns I had grown up in, on the eastern part of the state, were anyplace glamorous. Not to mention, Celine's jaw stays clamped shut until we've gotten back in the truck at the rest area and are in the remaining leg of our journey.

Driving the final stretch of road, the insane quiet is killing me. I haven't encouraged any small talk so she's not any more uncomfortable than her past seems to make her. Chances are I'd fumble my sentences in an effort to set her at ease and leave us both feeling embarrassed.

We wind through Boone. The sky has gotten darker as the sun's dipped on the other side of the mountains. Celine notes the lack of local college kids at this hour. They're either in the dorms studying hard or a bar drinking harder.

My place takes a few stoplights and turns to get to before a decent quiet stretch of trees line the road again. The silvery shimmer of headlights reflect off of mailboxes. The way they pop up out of the midnight blue makes it easy to forget it's only past suppertime. I spin the wheel one last time between the markers leading onto my property. After fifty feet, the trees clear. It gives me a three-sixty view to watch my daughter when she's playing outside. The porch light highlights the local mason's stonework on the chimney. Unfortunately, melting snow clings to the barren hedges I planted last fall. Someday, with the help of Skye's investments, it will be more.

Cece's eyes track across the yard. "This is amazing," she gasps.

Chapter Fourteen

Dusty

Her reaction has my chest puffing out. "It's paid for. I'd like to expand it someday." That's why it isn't up to snuff as far as I'm concerned. The place is still a work in progress.

I shouldn't be ashamed since the house still qualifies as brand-spankin' new. I worked with an architect who suggested the modular plan. It moved us in faster and we've been able to enjoy more seasons in the mountains. The same firm has concept drawings for the next phase, another reason why so much land is cleared.

I lead Celine inside, flipping on lights, and stay on the wide pine flooring in the kitchen while she takes in the open concept. Right now it's sort of a box. The bedrooms and bath take up about a third of the space with a balcony on top overlooking the living room and kitchen.

"There will be a second floor off the far wall."

Her mouth gapes open as she delicately touches a stone fireplace. "You'd take this out?"

"Add to it." I swoop my hand as if painting her a picture. "Make this bigger, so we have a real dining room instead of eat-in. Stairs over a garage." I haven't been able to decide how many stalls or if I want a woodshed attached. I suppose how fast my mind is made up has more to do with when we outgrow the space we do have. I'm not into showmanship. Yet, I want a place I want to come to and one I don't have to leave if I don't want to.

"Make yourself at home." I shoot off a text to Renata, letting her know we got here safe, and power off my phone before tramping back outside to collect our things.

"I can help," Cece calls after me.

"Your shoes are already off." I won't make light of it, but the measure of respect she has for the plush carpeting is more than my kid shows. I crank the heat, leaving the door open as I wander back and forth. On the final trip inside, I heft a cooler filled with food for the weekend onto the kitchen counter. Cece is peering out the windows and at the framed pictures of me and Sylvie skiing and playing outside in the snow.

"None of Beth?" she remarks as I stroll across the room.

"Bought this land after the accident with settlement money. Wanted a place to come and create new memories." I dig my hands in my pockets, locking my elbows.

Renata has tons of snapshots of Beth at home. Sylvie is a walking reminder of her mother. I'll always love Beth. However, I don't need to fill this space with the ghost of what might have been. For me at least, this spot in the mountains is what it is; a chance for my daughter and me to move on. I only want happy times for my little girl here.

"Sylvie is a total snow bunny." I point at a more recent image. "Swear that girl skis circles around me." I shake my head, letting out a lighthearted chuckle. "Renata even has it on video."

"You ski?"

"Yeah, had a few broken bones and wanted to prove I could still do something physical afterward. Sylvie and I learned together." She'd taken to it faster because kids are fearless.

Cece turns to me with a shy smile. "There's so much I don't know about you."

"There's a lot more I want to discover about you." I'm gentle, tucking a dark lock behind her ear and bringing her sweet lips to mine. No teeth. No tongue. No diving in like a man starving for his next breath. Pulling away a moment later, a blush rises from her neck, seeping to her cheeks.

"You've never kissed me like that."

"Haven't had much of a chance, now have I? Lemme change that, Cees."

She bites her lip, trying not to smile too broadly, and lowers her gaze, taking in the way my shirt stretches at the collar.

"Is there anything left in the truck? Do you need me to unpack the things for the fridge?" Her eyelashes flutter.

I haven't seen this side of Cece. She's embarrassed by true affection and doesn't know how to handle me being upfront about the way I feel about her.

"Nah. There'll be plenty of other chances to help. Relax. You're my guest and it was a long haul to get here."

Cece finds the bathroom and checks out Sylvie's room. The frilly pink comforter on the double bed makes her joke about finally understanding my quip about the princess mafia.

"Aidy helped buy all that stuff," I say.

"My brother has been here?" she asks in a wondering tone.

I figured she'd been told. The tendency a lot of us have to keep personal shit private isn't unusual because of Carver and Trig's business interests. You learn not to question certain aspects at the mill. Cece doesn't seem offended, and it rolls off her back.

"Yeah, Morgan and Aidy came while I was decorating." I wanted the room to be a surprise for Sylvie, but hadn't known what to do when I couldn't find character bedding in anything but twin size. "Aidy did all the feminine stuff with crowns and lace. She added the pictures, dolls, and pillows of her favorite characters... Your brother had a heck of a time sleeping in here when it was all done."

"Too girlie?" She giggles.

"It gave him a taste of what's on the hor-rizon."

"Ah, Morgan will get over his anxiety once he and Aidy take the next step. He worries too much about keeping people safe."

"We all do," I agree.

Cece tries to pass by me. I hook a finger into her belt loop and wrap my arms around her middle. We left-foot right-foot the few paces to the opposite room. Stopping by the bed, Cece's kneecaps hit the mattress. I cage her in, pressing my body to her back.

She's so quiet I can hear the rustling of the trees outside. I move her hair to one side, kissing her behind the ear. She always smells like a summer herb garden and fresh starts.

"Steam's coming out your ears, Cees." What's on her mind?

"This is a *really* big bed."

My chest rumbles. "I'm a big guy."

"Yeah, you are." She turns in my arms. I squeeze her ass so Cece feels how her words affect me. "We've never... in a bed."

"There hasn't been enough time." Plus, we were already breaking the golden rule, screwing in the ladies' bathroom. I wasn't about to step into Cece's bedroom, even if I did have to stop myself every damn time I passed her door. "You want to?"

"What do you want?"

Every damn piece of you. I hide my internal growl.

The demure act Cece's playing isn't part of her stage show. It's a fucking turn on, nonetheless. "Get on your knees."

She sinks to the carpet on command and my dick's jumping to attention before her dainty fingers have dragged my jeans to my ankles. She's about to make a comment about me taking her first date suggestion to heart.

"No boxers." I beat her to the punchline. "This weekend you have an all-access pass."

Cum is already boiling in my balls when she cups them, using her other hand to stroke my long length. "Open up, Cees. It ain't going to suck itself and there's not a part of you that doesn't belong wrapped around my cock."

She licks me from the root, teasing her tongue up my shaft before the tip disappears between her lips. I cup the back of her head, tangling my fingers in her hair, watching her struggle to take all of me to the back of her throat.

The only better visual is the day I lifted Cece onto the bathroom sinks, spread her knees wide, and we stared where our bodies were joined. I slid in and out of her with slow steady strokes, both of us fighting off our orgasms.

Once Cece comes, all I want is to unload all I've got inside of her. She's a refuge from my shitty past. A reminder I'm not letting anything stop me from putting back the pieces. I may never be the guy I once was, with the big deal degree and white-collar job. But it doesn't mean I don't like the man I am today. Or I'm incapable of giving the people I care most for the life they deserve.

It's not sissy, stalker-obsessed, love-sick bullshit to believe what lies ahead includes Celine Wescott. She stopped me in my tracks the first time I saw her dance. Knowing she was a mill girl—someone working toward a better future—was what prompted me to chase her.

And if we fuck this good? There has to be more to layer on top.

Cece has one hand stroking with a twist. Her hungry lips suck me while her hums of pleasure make me sure she's enjoying this as much as I am. Her other fingers are massaging the sweet spot behind my balls. She figured out almost off the bat it drives me wild. Looking at me under veiled eyelashes, both of Cece's hands move, sliding across my hips, gripping my ass. She lets me drive into her mouth while I cradle her chin in my palms. A million other guys would pay to be in my shoes. She trusts I won't hurt her, use her, and that's what had me falling for her. I don't take the gift of faith lightly.

Her fingertips spread my ass cheeks and we venture into new territory.

"Do that," I hiss, every part of my body clenching in anticipation, "and you'd better be prepared to swallow all of my cum down." My jaw locks, but I manage to grit out, "Not an ounce falls from those beautiful lips."

Cece gives me a soft nod. There's the slightest bit of apprehension in the way her body stiffens. It's no different than the way she acts whenever we've explored quick ways to get the other off. She wouldn't have dared suggest it otherwise. If she wants this power over me, I don't mind giving it to her either.

"Nobody's had me since you came around, Cees." I brush a knuckle against her chin, still supporting her neck. "Be prepared. Not a single drop."

She answers by pushing in. I detonate on contact, letting go in a way I can't begin to describe. I'm guilty of moving my grip to Cece's face and fucking her mouth like an animal. She's doing her best to swallow me down, but where I haven't had a damn lot of time in recent days for the images she leaves in my spank bank, I don't want her choking.

My legs are weak, but I pull her up from her knees. There's a droplet on her lower lip. I touch it, spreading the wetness like a gloss. Her tongue flicks out and her teeth scrape it back into her mouth. It's the sexiest thing I've ever seen.

My thumbs skim up, caressing the underside of her breasts, cursing the shirt she's still got on.

"I'm at a disadvantage. I've never seen you naked," she whispers.

"You wanna change that?" I kick off my shoes and my lips tickle behind her ear.

"How do you manage doing two things at once?" She squirms as my arms wrap around her waist.

"Practice. Have to make every minute with you count." I whip my tee over my head. "Advantage Celine." I tease, reaching for the buttons on her shirt. I'm in the buff. Cece's able to walk out of here. Though given the way her eyes graze over me, I'm placing bets she'd look back.

Cece clamps my hand to her chest. "Do you, um, want me to do it?"

I'm not fumbling with the buttons, so it takes me a second to catch her meaning. "You want to strip for me?"

My harsh tone has her mortified. "You've watched," she remarks. "I thought it turned you on."

She's not wrong but, "Sometimes the fun part is unwrapping the gift."

"You already know what's underneath."

"Yeah, Cees, I do." And it's up to me to convince her she's more than she sees.

Chapter Fifteen

Celine

Dusty's hand wraps around my hair, tugging my face close to his. His lips assault mine and the sudden unfounded fear I had that he wouldn't desire me because I've used my body to earn an income vanishes.

I'd wanted to give Dusty a private show as a thank you. And maybe to watch his reaction.

Would he sit in the chair and admire me appreciatively? Or would his hand snake down his pants, jacking his cock, teasing me the way I torture him. Because we both know how fucking amazing it feels when he strokes me on the inside.

It was also a way of proving he was a little more special than the other guys who've watched me take off my clothes. Up on stage, the light shining in my eyes left me blind to those men. There were some nights I knew Dusty was out there, leaning against a wall past the audience. On those evenings I danced for him. Not that he's ever known. It's not a detail we'd share rutting in a ladies' room. Yet, if I wanted to feel sexy when I'd spent my last bit of energy on sex appeal, it was Dusty who seized my thoughts.

My hands hang at my sides as Dusty undresses me. My pulse pounds and my fingers tremble the way they do when I'm past starving. The button down blouse slides off my shoulders. He flicks the clasp on my bra. The bands and cups fall forward. I catch them in my hands, pressing the silky fabric back, covering my nipples so I'm less exposed. I'm not sure what's brought on my modesty. He's seen it all.

Dusty should be the one concerned standing naked before me for the first time. He's unashamed of his body. The fine scars from broken glass covering his forearms are similar to ones on his thighs. His knee—a joint I've never laid my eyes on for the number of times I've enjoyed the sight of that other part of his body—has deep scars and is fingerprinted by the shadow of old staples. On anyone else, it's unremarkable. Yet, Dusty is a man torn apart and rebuilt. Whatever version I'm getting, the doctors only used the best parts.

My pants shimmy down my legs, I step on the hem, removing my socks with my feet.

Every caress is reverent. I feel... valued. It's strange and unfamiliar. I've spent the past months convincing myself I'm nothing but a detour in Dusty's day. A way for him to get his jollies. And because I didn't stop it, I condemned myself for leaning into his touch. For desiring him. And for being secretive about our connection. The less I spoke, the more material the lies became. My promiscuity. His aptitude.

I'm sensing we've both hidden behind the truth. I still may be doing it as a defense mechanism.

Slow doesn't mean simpleminded. And I could never consider Dusty uncaring. I've never felt like less of a tramp than I do right now.

My bra tumbles to the carpet. "What do you want from me?"

"A chance."

"For what?"

"All the stuff you haven't given me yet." His dark eyes with wide pupils search my face. "Cees, don't let anything stop this." He brushes my hair behind my ear. "We're already bigger than whatever you think we are."

My mind circles around his words as Dusty lowers me to the bed. Everything about him is larger than life. Why would his sentiments be any less? Because I hadn't given him credit for being a whole person until he'd asked me out is why. After dismissing the parts of him that I didn't use for so many months, I was ashamed of my behavior. Even more so than my self-criticisms engaging in a relationship the crux of which was getting the other off.

His hands splay my knees and even before his lips trail the insides of my thighs my back is arching in anticipation. Dusty's fingers spread my folds. He flattens his tongue, licking me from back to front. I know what's coming as he sucks the tiny ball of nerves into his mouth. He's done this to me before. A few of the best times not asking me to return the favor before unlocking the door and moving on to the next task in his day.

My legs would wind in the sheets if we'd pulled the comforter back. His strong palms hold me open, savoring on my pinkest parts as if my pussy is the cream on the dessert he shared on our date.

I wrap my hands around the pillows above my head. I'm searching for purchase, something to hold on to steady my incoherent mind. I bring the sham down over my eyes to silence the reasons for considering a relationship with him wrong.

Dusty's forearm bats the pillow off of the bed. I moan and he growls, enjoying the sounds I make. His tongue is relentless, bringing me to the cusp, and making me shatter.

I want him inside of me, but Dusty's not done

making sure I'm thoroughly ravaged. His fingers replace his tongue, slicking one to press farther back. I mewl at the tight invasion. Visions of doing the same to Dusty swirl in my head; how hot it was when he'd given me dominion over his body. His roaring release: The end result of pent up desire and frustration being without each other has caused.

His thumb rises up, stroking my clit. The build again is so intense. I'm reaching down this time, riding a wave of pure bliss. My hands tug at his shoulders. Like a rock, Dusty doesn't move more than replacing his thumb with his lips. My fingers tangle in his cropped dark hair, fucking his face, screaming out, cresting over the peak.

He draws out the last of my orgasm until my body goes limp and my knees shake. My energy depleted, they fall to the bed like molasses.

"Was that everything?" I'm panting and need a few minutes to recover, but I sure hope this isn't the end for today.

Dusty stands at the footboard, using his wrists to wipe the wetness from his face. I get no response. He turns, giving me a pleasurable view of his firm ass, and walks out into the kitchen. I hear the content on the fridge door clatter, a crisp sizzle-clink of a beer bolt opening, and the cap landing on a hard surface. He returns to the bedroom, proud cock on display, and the bottle's neck empty.

There's a lazy smile on his face as he watches me. I'm a puddle of goo and, rest assured, he's positive his magic's melted me.

"Never asked," he comments between sips, "just assumed all this" he motions towards the bed and my reclining form, "was as good for you as it is for me."

"It is."

He hums, clearing his throat. "Glad the problem's solved."

Dusty crawls back up the bed, leaving a slick trail up my midsection with his tongue. He worships each breast, sucking my still tight nipples into his mouth. Finally coming to rest on his side next to me, he places his head in his hand and turns me to face him. The tangy taste of beer tickles my tastebuds as we kiss. Dusty pulls back before I do.

"Why did you ask?" I caress his cheek.

"We fuck and we're done." He holds my hand up before it falls back to my chest. "I leave. You leave."

"I come back for more. You come back for more," I counter, despite it being the somewhat opposite. He comes to me.

"Can't blame a man for wanting to know." His tone is abashed. Unlike the strong and steady outside, inside Dusty's soft. He cares. I get the impression his curiosity is part male ego and as much ensuring he hasn't been careless of my feelings.

"Why do you come back? I mean, I won't look at a bathroom the same way ever again, but—"

"Did I have another option?" He cuts me off.

I trace his jawline. "I don't know. Not in the beginning. I was so mad at you."

"Why?"

"You got me all ramped up, kissing me, and didn't even come inside that night. Then, days later, you go off half-cocked on a customer as if we'd been in a relationship when you'd ignored me. I was so hurt and angry over the mixed signals. Plus, the next thing I knew we were all over one another with my bare ass sitting on the cold sink." My hands flail and he cuffs both, stilling them.

When we're intimate, the tighter he holds, the better it is. But this sensation isn't sexual in nature. A fist squeezes my lungs and my heart beats like a savage animal trying to break free of a cage.

"You wanted me to come in?"

My mouth twitches and I give Dusty a "you've gotta be kidding me" look. "I guess by the time you finally were inside with me, I figured it was how you did relationships.

"Not at all. Thought you wanted to hang with Skye. By the time the guy at Sweet Caroline's wouldn't let you alone, my jealousy got the best of me."

"You were there in the parking lot? I did kiss you back." The sarcasm has a twinge of amusement to it.

"*You* ran out soon as you saw Holly as compet-ti-tion."

We stare at one another for a moment and the air shifts. For as magnetic as our attraction has been, we've done a bang-up job of trying to jam like poles together and letting them push off one another. Better than a year's worth of misunderstandings click.

"Maybe if I'd explained," I say sheepishly.

"Forgivenesses' not a one-way street."

"You have to stop letting me off the hook. It's becoming a problem." Not communicating is both our faults. However, I need the Dusty who didn't back down from what he wanted when he sought me out as much as I do this version of him. I hate to admit the gruffness was as attractive as it was. Not that I want to be dominated, but challenged? Hell, yeah.

"Okay. From here on out, then. Higher standard." Dusty rolls on top of me, framing my face with his arms.

Chapter Sixteen

Dusty

I may have died and woken up in heaven. Celine and I did what we do best until exhaustion overtook us. The sheets are knotted everywhere—the fitted one has even come loose—and the comforter fell on the floor sometime after midnight. Cees is in the fetal position and the heat from my body curled around her has roasted us. I get up, admiring how beautiful she is naked in my bed, before finding something to cover her with.

My stomach growls as I pull on my boxer briefs and walk out of the room. We'd had dinner in bed, but expending all my energy, free to explore her body and savoring the slowness in a way we've never been able to before, has me hungry as an elephant. I have to replace those lost calories before doing anything today, including taking Cece back in there for round two.

I flip open the cooler, tossing the rest of the food I'd packed into the fridge. The mostly melted block of ice keeping it cold tumbles into the stainless steel kitchen sink, clattering louder than I'd like it to have. Water slops everywhere. I grimace, hoping the noise hasn't woken Cece.

When I spin around to close the fridge, she's standing in the threshold wearing the forest green sheet I'd tucked around her like a gown. Her head is tilted as if she's been watching me.

"I got cold. Your spot hadn't cooled. But it's not warm enough."

"Came out a minute ago to make breakfast." I run my palms over her upper arms. She's still toasty.

"I could do breakfast."

"Problem. We're out of eggs. Forgot Renata and Sylvie made cookies last weekend."

"You're here a lot?"

"As often as we can. No reason to have the place otherwise… Gotta make a run to the store."

"Let me get dressed and I'll come with you."

"Sure?"

She nods her head, running a fingertip down my forearm. My skin catches fire when she does that.

I'm impressed Cece is a quick-change artist. She's got her jeans on with a v-neck tee and her hair under a ball cap ready to leave before I've gotten my teeth brushed. I guess I'm used to my kid dawdling and figured she'd need more time before snagging her coat.

We're in the dairy section at the grocery store before we know it. I open the refrigerated case, inspecting several in a carton of eggs and ensuring none have cracks before placing them in the basket.

"Bacon?" Cees points to a microwave package display nearby.

"Have plenty."

"Thank goodness. Aidy is a bacon fiend. We always make extra when she's around so we get some. I wasn't sure if you were the same."

My lip quirks. "I'll share mine if you need more."

"Thank you." Her response to my generosity comes

out soft and her cheeks start to pinken. "I may have underestimated that a burly guy would be such a giver... in so many ways." She rises on her toes to press her lips to mine. I have to tip the brim of her hat up so it doesn't hit me in the forehead and am rewarded with the minty fresh taste of her toothpaste.

Certain we only need eggs, it's proven I'm out of my element shopping with a woman. Cece glances at the next row of freezer cases. "Do we need ice cream?"

"For breakfast?"

"Dessert. Um, what's for dinner?"

"Grilling steaks."

"In the dark and in the cold?"

"Ice cream is cold." I shrug, cocking my chin at the half gallons. We amble across the aisle. "Don't mind standing on the porch alone."

"I can wear a sweater. Chocolate or vanilla?"

"Fudge Swirl. Peanut butter cup. What's that face for?" I ask when she wrinkles her nose.

"I don't like stuff in my ice cream. I don't even like stuff *on* my ice cream."

I chuckle, remembering when we were out to dinner she inquired if the plain chocolate cake was served with any other toppings. She's even bucked the idea of trying the whipped cream on mine until I'd force the spoon on her. I slide closer and move Cece's hair over her shoulder. "Last thing I'd have pegged you for was an ice cream virgin," I whisper in her ear.

Red seeps up from Cece's collar as heat floods her body. Her tongue licks out, touching her upper lip. My hand brushes her torso. I turn away, selecting a large, round tub of Neapolitan to satisfy both our cravings later on... What she's craving now? Well, we're not used to having one another whenever we damn well please, and that's best kept on a slow simmer today as well.

"Do you have plans for all that ice cream?" she flirts.

I'm three paces ahead of her on the way to the checkout, getting a kick out of Cece chasing me for once. "Yeah, I'm eating it. In a bowl. With a spoon. Remember, you don't like stuff *in* or *on* it." I wink.

She stops in her tracks and starts laughing. By the time she's done being doubled over, she has to jog to catch up to me at the register.

"I'm not that funny."

"No, but we are. This side of you isn't what I'm used to, and I was more laughing at myself." She sidles past me to bag our purchases. "Paper or plastic?"

I choose paper as the cashier inquires cash or charge. I hold up my card and slide it through the reader. Cece studies me with intent. Taking the sack from her, and Cees by the hand, I carry it out to the truck.

"Are you afraid I'll get lost in the parking lot?" She kicks a fat tire.

"Force of habit." I stow the groceries behind her seat.

"Trucks or motorcycles?"

"Trig and the boys can keep their bikes." I open her door so she can climb in. She's more adept in pants than a skirt. I shake my head, walking around the front since I'd had to stop from doing more than admire the view. I like the way her ass looks getting in the truck no matter what she's got on.

"Would you have rather had sausage?"

"No. Bacon is messy to cook, but tastes great." I fire up the engine. "Why the twenty questions?"

"I realized there's a lot we don't know about one another. Isn't it why you asked me to come away with you this weekend?"

I don't reply. Instead, my right palm rests on her thigh and I squeeze before peppering her with similar either-or questions.

Back at the house, Cees starts the coffee maker and I scramble the eggs. She's eager to assist me, but I signal I've got it handled. She opts to take her mug and sit on the couch, updating charts.

We're hungry, though I take my time buttering the toast and frying bacon. I steal glances across the room. She's deep in thought and her nails *clickity-clack* over the keyboard.

I don't miss paperwork or e-mails or endless meetings where everyone says they're doing something important, but it's actually a wasted hour and an excuse to eat a dozen glazed donuts. I'm sure Cece's enjoying her work and that's what makes it worthwhile. Not having that same sense of fulfillment is how I knew it was time to pop the parachute and let rocket science land back on earth with grace, instead of watching my career implode on the launchpad.

As I'm getting plates from the upper cabinet, Cece logs off and turns on the radio. Not bothering to adjust the tuner, a sultry Santana melody fills the space. Her foot taps and her hips sway in time with the beat. I watch mesmerized like I've done at the club as her hands run up her silhouette and find their way into her hair. I'm not sure she's aware I'm still in the room when her head lolls back on her shoulders, but then she cha-cha's, her knees bending, able to keep her balance as she slinks toward me.

When she's close enough to tug into my space, my palm encases her middle, bringing Celine tight against me. Joined at the hip, my right foot moves forward and her left goes back. She reaches up to place one hand on my shoulder. The other goes for my forearm and her nails tickle my bare skin.

"You can dance!" She's excited.

I use the hand on her hip to twirl her and she spins back. Our fingers intertwine, palms together. Feet moving in rhythm to the smooth sound.

"Haven't in a longer than I'd like to admit. No good reason to."

"Am I a good reason?" She fishes for a compliment

when I've already given it to her. I spin her again to keep her on her toes and wrap my arms around her as her back hits my chest. We rock back-and-forth as the music fades into the next song.

"Were you a ballerina?" I have my nose tucked to her neck, inhaling the sweet smell of us still on her skin.

"Only in my pink-slippered, button-nosed dreams." She sighs. "My parents didn't have money for lessons, but I loved watching people dance on TV and in the movies."

"So how'd you become a dancer?"

"A girlfriend and I snuck out and went clubbing when we were teens. I was at a bar in Raleigh when someone suggested I dance for real."

"With your clothes off?"

"No." Her hand leaves my arm, momentarily waving off the way I tease her. She smiles at me and looks to where I hold her across her middle. "I'm guessing they meant like you'd see in a video or at a concert, but a lot of those background dancers have serious resumes. It's pretty competitive. I hadn't given it a second thought until my rent went up and my roommate stiffed me for her part of the utilities. Lamps don't glow if the power company shuts the lights off, and it's hard to study in the dark. I also needed patient contact hours in a nursing facility so I didn't have to take a gap year before PA school and working a third job made undergrad almost impossible. There weren't enough hours in the day."

"I'm sorry."

"I'm not. She was a sloppy bitch. Though, I suppose living with a crappy roommate is better than living on the streets. Anyway, at the same time I'd driven by Sweet Caroline's. Jake had a sign out front they were hiring and the pay was better than what I was making combined. I had nothing to lose, other than my apartment, which isn't saying much. So I danced for him and he gave me the job." Cece laughs again, wiggling against my tightened grip to turn and face me. "I said I danced for him, not I fucked Jake, Dusty."

"I'm sorry," I repeat. "I don't know—" *didn't know?* My jaw cracks. My brain and my emotions are at odds, and I'm not sure I used the right context.

"How I got started? What's with that bulging vein in your neck? This is the same vibe you gave off to the club's clientele when you'd go all *Incredible Hulk.*"

"You thought I wouldn't be jealous." It's said stern.

"Of course, I expected something. But I counted on you trusting I wasn't fucking anyone else. In the beginning, I had to have a little faith it was the same for you, or else—"

She shrugs and I scrub my face, finishing her sentence, "You'd think I believe you were a—"

"Complete and total slut."

I cup her cheek, bringing my forehead to hers. Closing my eyes, I pray she'll see past my insecurities.

"Stripping didn't turn me on, Dusty. It was a means to an end. The audience was in the dark, and I couldn't see past the stage. I concentrated on the next move, never considering what I was doing to get them off."

"They were all going home adjusting hard-ons, same as me."

Cece bites then licks her lower lip and I tilt my head as to ask "What?"

"I wondered if you'd come find me on the nights you were at Sweet Caroline's or if I'd be stuck waiting for the next afternoon."

I'd always stayed to the shadows as not to get Cece in any trouble. "You didn't like me making you wait."

"No. But you always made it worth the wait."

Chapter Seventeen

Celine

We're still standing in the kitchen and Dusty's about to plate the bacon.

"This smells delicious," I say. "Why hasn't anyone snapped you up yet? Women love men who can cook."

He doesn't mean to come off as snarky, but the jovial sarcasm is blatant as it can be. "Most women aren't interested in my kind of baggage. I'm a single dad. Living in my not-quite mother-in-law's spare room. Top it off by waiting to get custody of my daughter? Not the hottest commodity, Cees."

We both look to where I'm holding onto his bicep. My fingers don't match half the circumference. Glancing up, our eyes meet and Dusty sighs. For a split second, I see the way he views himself through the lens of others. He's an enormous presence. Reserved, like holding back a bear. The accident didn't take his mental acuity, but his delayed speech makes it seem so.

Without understanding how much heart lies beneath his wall of chest, it is a lot for any woman to digest. It was a lot for me. I allowed myself to only see what was on the surface because the shallowness was a layer of protection. Now that we're getting to know one another, I'm glad Dusty's given me a glimpse into his soul.

I pick up a slice of bacon, breaking it in half and feeding him a piece. "You're wrong. You are a very hot commodity." The tip of my finger disappears between his lips. Dusty holds my hand up. After he's done chewing, he licks away the salt.

"Eat up, Cees. I've got plans for you after this."

My eyes drift to the bedroom, remembering the way his body cocooned around mine last night. I am surprised at how comfortable it was sharing a bed when I'm used to sleeping alone. We were up late and a mid-morning nap after nookie sounds pleasurable.

However, Dusty's plans aren't quite as provocative as his words lead me to believe. We've hardly placed the dishes in the sink when he's bundling me up with extra socks, wrapping a scarf around my neck, and pulling a pink and purple striped stocking cap over my ears.

"Is this Sylvie's?" I touch the intricate crown embroidery.

He smirks, tying his boots, and grabs what looks like four tennis rackets from the closet, putting two under each armpit.

"Take these," he instructs me, relinquishing the skinny trekking poles. "Not going far, but you may need them."

"Me?"

"Novice. Hence, why we're staying in the woods around the per-rimiter. Don't need as much gear and less likely to get lost. Outside." He points to the door when the velcro on my gloves is secure.

There's a rustic country feel to being out in the middle of nowhere. The darkness last night hadn't given me a good glimpse of Dusty's property. Returning from the store this morning, the house sitting dwarfed in the center of a wide field surprised me. This mountain home isn't a cabin, and it's definitely not one of the cookie-cutter gabled suburban boxes found in Kimber and Trig's neighborhood. Inside and out, it's comfortable with contemporary lines, and I can visualize how beautiful it will be with the addition.

It's mild and sunny, but a slight wind whips at my pants. Let's face it, I'm a wimp when it comes to winter weather and am thankful for the short season on the other end of the state.

"Cold?" Dusty caught sight of my fists and spine tightening when the breeze blew over the field. "Had it snowed overnight, I would have broken out the ski pants."

Swirls of white cover the field with interspersed patches of grass showing dormant tips. A few areas the sun glints off of and I can tell it's icy. Others, closer to the tree line, have deeper mounds where the snow has built up over the past months and the overhanging conifer boughs haven't let the light in.

"I'll be okay once we're hiking around." I muse in a cheerful tone, up for the adventure.

"We won't be out too long. Plus, I got a way to warm you when we're through." Dusty winks with a devilish promise, dropping the snowshoes on the ground. He lifts my left boot, sliding the first one under like a slipper, and instructs me on how to tighten the straps. Much like at Royce's, he's using one-word cues and counts the steps with his gloved fingers. Once it's secure, he makes me do the right snowshoe myself while he dons his own pair.

We walk around the house first. It's built with a sloped backyard, and I'm stunned at how high the porch off of the back actually is. From the living room the expanse of white yard had given the illusion of being much closer to the ground.

"Know what a flag lot is?" he asks.

"Nope. But I'm sure you'll fill me in."

"I have an easement between two other lots to get to my land. This whole side," he swoops an arm, "is a straight line boundary all the way back. The other, where you can make out the back of the neighbor's house, comes in at an L-shape." He maps it out with his hands. "Most people want property adjace-nt to the road."

"It didn't bother you."

"I come here for seclusion." He chuckles. "Jake joked I should build a compound."

"Like the mill isn't one."

"No kidding."

"Has he been up here?"

"No. He set me up with the right people to get the sale and permits approved."

My brow furrows.

"Jake's a man of hidden talents. If anyone mentions his golf game needs work, it's a hustle. He knows what he's doing."

I shrug and leave it at that.

With my feet set wide apart, walking toward the straight tree line is harder than it looked on the YouTube video I watched after Dusty invited me up here. He gives me a pole to steady my balance in the frosty thicket, mentioning he's keeping the second for himself out of an extreme amount of caution in case he hits an icy patch.

"Rehab from breaking a bone, it makes you never want to break anything again."

Before this past week, we knew nothing about each other beyond the carnal. I like Dusty's honesty, his willingness to open up to me, and his humor. I find the stutter endearing because it shows how hard he tries not to give up on the person he was. Dusty values those ten cent words, wants them to flow the way they used to, and isn't afraid to put in the efforts so they will.

He's proving a much more whole human being than I am. The more time I spend in his company, the more it highlights the flaws in the hard-lined schedule I'd sketched out for my life.

We weave in and around tree trunks, never venturing far from the clearing. I concentrate too much on my footsteps and he encourages me to look up into the canopy. The air we breathe is icy, warming as it enters our lungs, and creating foggy puffs with each exhale. My heart pounds and I lose my breath laughing when we make goofy smoke puffs. Dusty's practiced to entertain his little girl and creates the circular ones with holes in the center.

"Could you do this someplace more rugged? The resort a few miles down the road has cross-country skiing too."

"You could persuade me to figure it out. Another time?"

A glow radiating from his face outshines the one he's put on mine. It's hard to hold hands with thick gloves on, but our outstretched arms connect, anchoring us together on the way back inside.

We shed everything covering our feet at the door and hang our coats and gloves. The heat of the wood stove sends prickles over my skin. My muscles are warm underneath. Zips and shocks run through my system. The odd cozy and sleepy sensation you get after Thanksgiving dinner takes over.

"You okay?" Dusty snakes a finger into the belt loop in my jeans, stopping me from toppling over as I take off my sock. The bottom got wet when I stepped in a puddle at the entry.

"Only winded." I place my palm on his forearm. I love the way they feel around me, keeping me safe from the smallest mishap. I swear he'd hold the safety net, ready to catch me, if I fell from a high wire. "Who knew that a month of no dance practice would leave me so out of shape? My clothes are a little more snug in the rear if you get my drift."

"Can I say something and you take it the way it's meant?" His lower jaw juts out and his tongue finds his back molar, tentative and pensive about what he's revealing.

"Sure."

"Warning you. I'm gonna blow this." He apologizes in advance. "I didn't know Beth's body before she was pregnant."

His palm glides over the bell of my hip and I look to where it stalls with a soft thumb rub over my belly button. Then I glance up at Dusty. His lips part as if he wants to take back bringing his ex up, but his meaning is clear before he stumbles to explain. And what's more, while it's still far off on my timeline of events, this is the first instance in my entire life the idea of having a baby isn't overwhelming.

"Beth always commented about what her ap-pearance was like before Sylvie. I had nothing to compare it to. She was perfect and you're perfect. An extra pound or lump doesn't change anything."

I turn and wrap my arms around his neck, brushing my fingertips across the scruff of his beard as I do. He leans into my touch. His hands grab my ass, squeezing, before settling his beefy palms at my waist.

"I might show up for a rehearsal or two at Sweet Caroline's. It's how Kimber stays in shape since she stopped dancing."

"Either way, do what's right for you. I'm not complaining."

I nod as Dusty's face lowers to mine, rubbing our noses together before the gentlest kiss.

"You didn't blow it bringing up Beth." I don't get the impression Dusty wants me to live up to a standard she set. The few times he's opened up about his past have had more to do with his own experiences.

"Thank fuck!" He tosses his head back and lets out an enormous growling sigh, lifting me off the floor.

"Were you that worried?" I tuck my ear to his chest, listening to his huge heart beating.

"You're the only person I've felt like this about since her, so yeah." He scrubs his beard. "Not supposed to say that so soon either, am I?"

I tighten my grip at his middle. "I feel it too." I stop and let out a self-conscious laugh. "Not the second time around part, though."

I don't take solace in the fact that I've been on my own so long this can't hurt when it ends. I'm not sure I've ever experienced anything other than puppy love or lusty obsession. Of course, they never live up to the fictionalized image of what I expected a man to behave like. I'll admit what's happening now is different. Sure Dusty's got rough edges, but he's so gentle, so caring, mine are more likely to stab him in the heart.

"It's more than what we were doing." I turn, resting my chin. This close I can see the gorgeous gold flecks in his brown eyes.

"So... Much... More." In between words, Dusty kisses my forehead.

Something inside of me swells and my world shifts. I have this moment where I know next weekend, the weekend after that, and a month from now, it'll be as amazing. I picture myself confiding in Sloan about how this man makes me feel. My mind's eye rushes on fast forward. I've got her and Carver along with me and Dusty meeting up with Trig and Kimber at the hole-in-the-wall Mongolian Barbecue—a restaurant so far on the other side of the dine-out spectrum from eating at Royce's—and running into my brother as he's grabbing takeout. It's all so normal, and so within my grasp, I can almost hear the sizzle of the grill and taste the food set in front of me.

I don't remember this insane happiness or

contentment, even when I walked across the stage for my diploma. Although methodical, I can't help wondering how worthwhile the stages of my plan are. If I shouldn't have thrown caution out the window, admitted my attraction to Dusty, and see where it led. My friends don't dislike him. The reservations I had were a combination of my own insecurities and unwillingness to check off the "fall in love" box before the "become a PA" one. The sequence didn't matter in the end. But I was too narrow-minded to recognize they both fulfilled the dream.

Chapter Eighteen

Celine

I have my legs tucked up on the sofa criss-cross with my laptop open on my lap. The heat from the battery has my bare, happy toes wiggling underneath and the fire across the room allowed me to shed my sweater a half hour ago when Dusty left to find the toolbox he keeps here. We're both tackling our to-do lists so we can go back to the good parts.

I hit save on the second to last chart. While waiting on the slower than molasses internet to open the next, I take the last big gulp of cocoa in my mug. The chocolate slides down my throat. Filling the kettle was not what I'd expected when Dusty said he'd "warm me up." He likes teasing me. But I yawned, tucked to his chest as we waited on the water to boil and he promised a naked nap in our future.

My cell rings next to me on the cushions, and pretty much the worst interruption ruins the rush of positivity coursing in my veins.

"Hi, Mom." It's better to answer than ignore. She'll keep hitting redial until I pick up. She must be making up for all the times over the years she hasn't called all at once.

"I saw your graduation picture on Facebook." She starts without any term of endearment. *Would opening with some sort of congratulations have killed her?* "You're a doctor now?"

"No. I'm a pediatric physician's assistant." My chin tips up, defiant. I hope big words throw Mom off, and I'm racking my brain as to how she wound up with the information. I have an unused in ages account. Someone at the ceremony in December must have tagged me in a photo. I'd stopped logging on for that reason. Everyone felt compelled to share news stories about my brother's sentencing. It was as if they'd forgotten I was front and center to the hell the legal system forced Morgan to endure.

"Same difference," she pshaws. "I saw a PA at the emergency room last month." She's begging for me to bite and be sympathetic to her plight. Too bad I'm onto what she's after.

My mother didn't use when Morgan and I were young. The first time I saw her drunk I was in middle school. Strung out happened a year or two later. The older we got the deeper her habits seemed to stretch. The more time alone with my bitter father, the more apparent her means of escape became. However, Morgan and I weren't in a position to intervene and call her on her habits. It was the point when we realized the only support network we had was one another.

It doesn't matter that we were adults when Morgan went to prison. I'm not sure how to forgive her for abandoning my brother and I when we needed a parent to lean on during the tough times. I also don't think I should have to.

On a scale of one to ten, my dad didn't start out as a complete zero. I remember him shooting hoops with Morgan, building my brother's skills early on.

Although, it was before he realized my brother was a decent enough player to go anywhere. He got a partial scholarship to the big-name university my dad obsessed over as *his team*, and had a shot at a better life.

We never had much. Mom—whose lack of education and skills made a series of fast food jobs she was fired from for missing work, her sole option for income—went along with everything he said like it was the gospel. She lost herself to him and, when Dad refused to be there as Morgan's dreams fell apart, Mom let Dad extinguish any hope she had left. I've come to the conclusion they stay married because neither is interested in the effort it takes to separate.

My nails dig into the flesh of my palms, reiterating to myself she's an ignorant product of her environment and knows no better. But Morgan and I were too, and we didn't roll over and give up. He'd never lay a hand on Aidy and I'd never allow addiction to stop me from loving.

She babbles on incoherently about an aunt whom I only know by name. "Did you hear me say I br..ke my arm?"

I've gotten off the couch and am pacing by the slider wearing a pattern in the carpet. The call has gone staticky and her voice choppy and robotic.

"No. You didn't mention it." I make the get on with it motion.

The call continues cutting in and out. "The doctor at the ER gave me pills for the pain, but he w..n't give me no more and it hurts so bad I can't h..rdly sleep." Mom suggests I report him to the state medical board.

"I can't, Mom," I remark, bored.

"Well, then can y...refill the pres...iption? The pharmacist s..."

The line goes dead right as I'm about to snap and give my mother a piece of my mind. It's not as if I hadn't figured out what she was after, but how dare anyone ask me to risk my license?

I stare at the screen incredulous. The low-battery icon flashes red from trying to hold the connection and drains the last drop of energy. My voicemail box will be full when it's juiced up again. But at least I have a valid reason for not answering.

I hit save and close my laptop. Unable to complete my task until I've cleared my head, I go fish through my purse for the charger and find it missing. Fuming at my stupidity for not packing it, I pinch the bridge of my nose, taking a few calming breaths. Regaining enough composure to act normal, I venture through the house to find Dusty in the bathroom.

"Hey," I wiggle my cell. "Have an extra phone cord by chance?"

Dusty is on his back under the sink. He peers out. "Not that brand."

"Awesome. It's dead and I forgot to pack mine."

"Happens out here. Shut mine down. Weaker signals."

"What if something happens while you're gone?"

"You mean with Sylvie? Renata and I have a deal that I check in every so often."

I nod at the sensibility of his plan and he offers to take a ride to the store to get a new cord.

"Nah." I slide down the wall to sit on the edge of the tub. The bright side of admitting defeat is putting my past behind me. I set my phone to the side.

"Done with charts?"

"One left. It's quick. I lost motivation and can have it finished before Monday."

Dusty nods, saying his own task is almost accomplished.

I pick up the empty box from the faucet he's installing. There's nothing wrong with the original one. He found one he likes better. It's pretty and rustic with white hot and cold disks on the handles.

Dusty's quiet, focused on his task under the sink. I've noticed he doesn't hold conversations while he does anything. In the beginning, it seemed as if he needed to concentrate, but then I realized how adept he actually is. His actions are no more delayed than mine. It's only obvious when he talks that anything is wrong. It takes him longer to form sentences. Sometimes, when they're more complex, he gets a thoughtful expression on his face. Not confused, as much as contemplative or deliberate, and there's an undeniable attractiveness to an intelligent man. During those moments, my patience with him increases because I honestly want him to say what's on his mind. I'm not sure if it will be smart, sexy, or comical. What I do know is it gives me more insight into how this man ticks.

"Why didn't you stay an engineer?"

It takes him a minute to speak. He stutters through it and there's a slight echo from his upper half resting inside the cabinet. Yet, having been around him most of the past few days, his words are as easy to understand as having a heart to heart with anyone else.

"The accident changed me. Realigned my priorities realizing nobody's guaranteed tomorrow. I went back for a while when I got off disability. I hadn't fit the mold to begin with. It wasn't worth the pressure trying to be the person everyone else needed to peg me as."

"How so?"

"Some, who'd given me credit beforehand, were overzealous. They didn't like thinking they'd been wrong. My brain injury had them recalculating. Others, who believed there was no way a guy who looked like me could be smart, felt vindicated. I was the butt of the joke."

"But these are adults. With advanced degrees!" I come to Dusty's defense.

These are the people you expect to know better. To be

role models for the rest of society.

He shimmies out, sitting up with tented knees. "If you can't accept intelligent people have preconceived notions, then you should look inside yourself. I'm not saying it to be a douche. I've fallen in that category too. What about you? Why did you go into medicine?"

"It's a convoluted story."

"Still want to hear it. Going someplace?"

"No, I'm right here." I put my elbows on my thighs and cross my arms. "The first one of my friends got pregnant when she was fifteen. Then they all sort of fell one by one. Some had babies before they graduated. Others had abortions just to get pregnant again. It was a fifty-fifty split. I didn't want that for me. I saw what it did to them. How it limited their choices. They had these beautiful little people to care for, but they were still kids too." The more babies surrounded me, the more homework I did on preventing myself from getting pregnant. I'd already decided I hadn't wanted the same outcome for me and made myself an appointment for birth control.

"They needed so much help. If I didn't find myself babysitting for free, then I was waiting by a stroller at the park while my friends duked it out with their baby daddies. Even the boys who stuck around caused more problems than they were worth. They hadn't wanted to be fathers to begin with. If my friends lived at home and hadn't dropped out, their boyfriends didn't get the exhaustion the moms faced being at school all day and caring for the baby at night. The guys wanted their girlfriends back—for it to be the carefree way it was when they were teens and not teen parents.

"I spend a lot of time drying tears, the moms' and the kids', and pocketing cough medicine because they got too close to getting caught the last time and never had the cash to take a sick baby to the doctor. You feel guilty because stealing isn't the help they need and things go from bad to worse. I had a close friend with a toddler who got pregnant a second time. Amy decided not to have the baby, but didn't tell her boyfriend until after. She had no choice because he was pressuring her into sex and she couldn't after the procedure. In between shaming her for being a so-called murderer, he beat Amy up. Their child was in the room. The neighbors called the police, which was what saved her. The EMTs wanted her to go to the hospital, but she had to choose between that and paying his bail for domestic assault. I wound up over there with leftover bandages from our medicine cabinet..." I let my voice trail. I don't want to tell Dusty the rest. This afternoon it hits too close to home.

"Anyhow, Morgan was a sure-win to get out of there whether he had a kid or not. Me? All I could do was pay attention in school and hope for the best." Becoming a doctor was out of my scope, but when I found out there was such a thing as a physician's assistant, it was where I set my sights.

"I'm proud of you for reaching your goal," Dusty says like he's watched me scale a lofty peak.

He has, though, hasn't he? I'd simply refused to look down as I climbed to listen for the silent cheers of the man rooting me on.

Chapter Nineteen

Dusty

"Oooh… Deeper," Cece moans.

My chest shakes as the meat of my palms press into her upper back. "Supposed to say that when I'm inside of you."

I'd meant it a little more seductive, but it makes her laugh. I'm beginning to like that response as much as the ones when she's moaning and writhing beneath me while I whisper dirty words in her ear.

Cees is anything but the quiet type when I get her off. At least whenever Cece has laughed, I haven't had to cover her mouth. It's a noise anyone can overhear and not pop an eyebrow over. Admittedly, the past few times I've brought her to the brink it's also been nice not to have to mask her cries of pleasure so they don't echo off the walls.

I'm not sure how she persuaded me to give her a back rub, but you'll hear no complaints from me. Cece is topless on the bed and I'm digging at knots between her shoulder blades. Her skin is soft, and I'd love to roll her over and see if she'll murmur these same words a little dirtier while I'm buried inside of her.

"Can't be doing everything right if you're this tense?"

She struggles to roll over and I lift my hips, putting my weight on my bad knee. Met by the sight of her glorious tits, the reward is well worth the tweak of pain.

"It's more the trip down memory lane. Talking about my past brings up too many negatives." She places her hands over mine as I massage up her torso and palm her breasts.

"Don't worry about that shit. It's long gone and you're unsto-p-pable." I release a sigh, wanting in this one instance to be more eloquent.

Double pronouncing the p right then was like coming too soon. Celine senses the turmoil caused by not being able to compliment her the way she deserves without stammering.

"Why don't you stutter when we're *together*?" One set of her fingertips move, dancing from my beard, down the thick column of my neck and playing with the chest hair surrounding my nipples.

"Shorter words and sentences." We touch one another in parallel, pinching, tweaking, caressing. "Also, may or may not have practiced."

"I may or may not need an explanation."

"Simple. Guys don't need to be descriptive asking for a blow." And if he's had his cock in his hand, fantasizing about driving his dick between anyplace on a lady, he's repeated the phrase he'll tell her in his head a million times.

She giggles and her belly goes concave, releasing pent up tension.

"I like you like this, Cees." I move again, pulling her knees apart and lowering my hips to hers, rocking into her pelvis.

"Half naked in your bed?"

"Happy… and topless… in my bed."

I cage her face in between my elbows, burying my nose into her long hair and sucking the sweet spot behind her ear.

Friction strains the denim seams of our jeans. The last time I dry humped a girl, I wasn't more than a boy. The corners of Cece's mouth turn up as her eyes close and she bites her lip. Her soft sounds grow louder. I'd forgotten how fun it was to get anyone off this way.

Impatient, she fumbles at my waistband. "Please."

"Beg," I demand.

"Fuck me."

"No." My lips torment hers with a slow, steady kiss. The rutting we'd done in my truck was an unexpected aftereffect from our month away from one another. Don't get me wrong, I thoroughly enjoyed the frenzied pace then and the one we kept while tangling up the sheets last night before passing out. But this kind of afternoon delight? I want to savor it or else I'd have bent Celine over the counter in the bathroom as soon as I finished installing the faucet. And I'm done with fucking her over a sink, unless we move on to the one in the kitchen. Now there's a thought to ponder. Plenty of flat surfaces in there to spread this woman out and feast on her bounty.

I lean back, popping the button on her pants and shimmy them down her legs. She's got on the thinnest pair of light pink underwear I've ever seen. The cleft of her pussy is visible, almost as if she's wearing nothing at all.

"Panties?" I'm shocked.

"This mountain man instructed me to cover my ass to stay warm."

I've got two hands ready and willing to heat up that ass. Overzealous stripping them off of her body, the edges fray. I hold them up.

"Oh, I was sort of into those. They fit nice and snug." Her head tilts on the pillow and she shoots me a devilish grin.

"Buying you more so I can take 'em off again… Know something else fits you 'snug' that'll make you feel nice?" I line my cock up with her entrance, pushing in leisurely to stretch her slick core.

Cees meets every stroke, lifting her pelvis as I rock into her.

This kind of pleasure doesn't happen all the time. There's hot and dirty fucking, makeup sex, and the instances your dick needs attention and the only true desire is getting your rocks off with a sure, easy lay. It's not been so long since I was in a relationship that I've dismissed those nights where the bump and grind of screwing is a box on your to-do list; Driven carpool, check. Worked out, check. Bought groceries, check. Banged your soon-to-be wife, check.

And then there's making love. The swivel of a woman's hips as you ride the apex of desire, urging one another on, giving and finding gratification in the torturous ride to the peak when you fracture, falling apart and climaxing.

It's been so long since I've had someone in my arms, wrapped around my body, whom I care this much about, that I can't help hungering for more. I want to take Cees higher. To make her scream louder. To feel her come and the rush of wetness drench my balls. My appetite was wet knowing my spunk lined her cunt, and now with the taste of it neverending? The potential for more has me craving all the things I swore I'd give her heart time to catch up with.

We tried "us" on for size the past few days. It's working. I'm ready for more and the way Cece claws at my shoulders and back as I drive us forward has me certain she's there too.

She quivers and tightens and I edge back, testing. Cece whimpers in response, clasping her palms against my face, and fusing our mouths. The kiss deepens and we lose ourselves. She cries out, arching her back. Her breasts rise. I suck one perfect taut nipple into my mouth, scraping my teeth against the tips while filling her with my cum.

"God, why is sex with you always so fantastic?" Cece pulls the sheet up to cover us, resting her head on my pec when I've rolled off of her.

Her tongue peeks out, licking the place on me that I've sucked on her.

She gets quiet while I catch my breath.

"Dusty?" She hesitates. "When you said last night it was only me, did you mean it?"

"Haven't been with anyone else since this started, no."

"Why? I'm the bathroom girl. I wouldn't know if you were telling the truth or not."

I roll to my side so she has to move too and tip her chin up with a knuckle, skimming her jawbone. "Didn't go into it with that intent. Thought I'd take you on a date sooner. Didn't happen."

"Why not?"

"Bathroom girl seemed happy with the way things were. If it was the only way I could have you—"

"You wanted us to be more like this?"

"Were you…" *with anyone else?*

"No!" She can't get the words out of her mouth fast enough. "I don't bed hop—even if we weren't doing it in a bed—I hadn't been with anyone in a while before you."

We're quiet for a second while how monogamous we've both been sinks in.

"Any reason?" I'm a dick for wanting reassurance only I can make her feel like this.

"Morgan's trial was distracting and grabby customers at Sweet Caroline's don't exactly spur your sex drive. Once you begin reading into why someone wants you, you sort of feel—I don't know exposed, dirty even, as if no one respects what you have to offer. And you try harder to prove the other things you're doing make you valuable."

"I'm sorry if I made you feel like that."

"Same goes for me, if you felt the same way. I wanted you to want me in all the right ways and still couldn't allow myself to think you actually did. The past week—this weekend especially—makes up for the months of limbo."

"For me too."

"What happens when we go home? What do we say?"

"We're no good at kiss-and-tell." I stop to gather the right phrase. "Per-haps we say we went out a few times, and it took longer to be sure we clicked." Our friends will rib us, but they're decent folk. They'll understand we hadn't wanted to disappoint or cause undue drama. "Let's leave what we were doing at the factory out of it." I sure as hell don't want anyone nicknaming her something as dismissive as *"bathroom girl"*.

"So we have a plan?"

"Assuming you're ready for everyone to know." I wait for confirmation.

"I do. Do you?"

"Hell, yeah." Thinking back, it's all I have wanted all this time but hadn't had the balls to ask for. I'd blame it on my limited experience with relationships over the past few years, putting my daughter first, and not finding the right person. But it goes deeper. When I'd found a woman I wanted to try again with, worrying Cece couldn't reciprocate put a crimp in my armor.

Getting to know how Celine ticks, a glimpse into her own insecurities, proves how misplaced the lack of confidence in myself was.

"Your ice cream purity is one of the saddest bedtime stories I've ever heard."

Our afternoon activities flowed past suppertime. Sustenance being of the utmost importance, we donned boots and jackets an hour ago to replace all those calories. I'm hoping we burn some of them off again later.

Even a big guy like me forgets how freeze-your-balls-off cold it is during the winter once the sun sets behind the mountains. True to her word, Cees stomped her feet to stay warm, while I tended to the grill. I kidded it was a damn good thing she'd packed more pairs of those paper-thin panties in her overnight bag to keep her ass warm. Then I snuggled her into my arms to maintain our body heat, teasing that her teeth-chattering company made it hard to understand what she was saying. It's easy not to take yourself too seriously when you're able to let your guard down.

After dinner, Cees scooped us both bowls of ice cream. Hers is vanilla. She made me choose a single flavor—I went with strawberry—and I swear she would have spooned off the infinitesimal bits of chocolate had I not intercepted the dish beforehand.

"There is nothing wrong with enjoying one thing at a time," she retorts.

I noticed her meat and veggies didn't touch. Her plate looked almost like those divided ones Sylvie had when my daughter was learning to feed herself.

I don't want to be an airplane spoon dad, but find myself holding up a utensil the way I had at the dessert bar in Raleigh. "Try this."

There was fudge in the back of the fridge. Who doesn't like chocolate covered strawberries, other than the woman wrinkling her nose and leaning away from the warm and melty bite of ice cold ice cream?

"Nope. Nope. Nope. No way. Get that out of my face." She mock bats at the food. Her lips seal shut, but the smile she's wearing lights up the dark places inside me, reviving a dormant part of my life.

I have no way to explain other than, you don't realize what you have until you lose it. Healing seals off a bit of that pain, so it doesn't hurt quite as bad. Then when the casket is cracked open again, the memory isn't agony, it's joy. It's like life hands you a drink toasting, "Hey, remember happiness? This was what that unabashed feeling was like. And you can still have it without all the suffering. You still deserve satisfaction without the strings of grief attached."

Chapter Twenty

I'm not sure which of the three of us—Cees, me, or my dick—was up first this morning, but we all appreciated the groggy waking while our limbs tangled together. The velvety softness of touching one another and spilling inside of her whenever I've pleased is something I'm ready to get used to.

It'll be weird sleeping alone tonight after I drop Cece off. However, we have the rest of the day and Cees seems as if she's in no rush to get home. Neither am I.

We're about to take up residence on the couch to figure out what to do with the day before having to pack up when she sights a bin of toys up on the balcony.

"Who is your favorite Disney Princess?"

She rests a knee on a cushion, straddling my hips. Her nightshirt, my shirt, rises. Cece sinks to my lap, the only fabric separating us is the flannel of my pajama bottoms.

"Don't have one." I tug her butt closer so that my cock rests where it belongs. I love my kid. Love that

Cees is comfortable asking about Sylvie. Right now, though the only person I want screaming "Daddy" is this woman.

"You have to. You have a daughter." She presses a hand to my chest to stop me from grinding up against her clit.

Is she serious? We've got about four hours, six max, and then we're saying goodbye.

"Okay, Cinderbelle." Cece looks at me like I've misspoken. "Maybe Sleeping Elsa?"

"There's no such characters. You tease Sylvie like this, don't you?" It dawns on her what I'm doing.

"Cees?"

"Yeah?"

"*Let it go.*"

She snorts, thumping a flat palm on my pec, and rolling her eyes. I hold it still as she compliments, "You're a good dad."

"Thanks. You like kids?"

"They're great."

"Want any of your own?" I'll give you a few. *Let's practice.*

"Someday." She shrugs and something inside of me shifts.

"Does that mean you aren't interested in coming back up here next weekend with me and Sylvie? You could bring your charts and I'll take her to the slopes while you work so we don't disturb you." Winter only lasts so long. I'd love to get a few runs in, bring my windburned-cheeked girl back here where we can spend some time together and she can get acquainted with Cece.

"Um, it may be too soon? A full weekend is a lot. I couldn't sleep in your bed, and she might have a lot of questions she'll be uncomfortable asking while I'm around."

"You're right." I scrub my face. I'm putting the cart

before the horse. Having them both here would combine the best of both my worlds. Renata said I needed to manage my relationships with both Sylvie and Celine. I'm tired of them being separate and since the lights went up signaling Celine's last night on stage, I've been ready to get on with my life.

"It's not that I'd never like to, Dusty. I would. It's just maybe when we finally do, it can start out smaller? Something local like the children's museum and then take Sylvie for chicken and waffles. Does she like breakfast for dinner as much as her dad?"

"She does." I kiss her temple. I'm disappointed, but she's trying to meet me halfway. "Do you eat chicken and waffles?" I nudge with a raised brow.

"Not together."

Her facial features scream it's an affront to nature, cracking me up.

"Why not?"

"Because, ew, maple syrup with fried chicken? That's like—"

"Ice cream with hot fudge?"

"Exactly!" Cece giggles, but I've watched the woman devour a salad. If she can put balsamic on greens, there's hope for her yet.

"You know what would go great covered in hot fudge?... An ice cream purist."

Her wild messy locks fan out in the air as Celine shakes her head, refusing. However, from the crimson seeping from the neckline of *my shirt that she's got on* and the glimmer in her eyes, the idea has merit. Cees isn't ready for me to wear her down, but considering the way she's kissing me, she's open to being worn out before our drive back to Brighton. One of us is going to have their mouths full soon, and knowing what she tastes like, I'm craving Cece.

I skim a knuckle down her front. The shirt indents when my finger hits her navel and I twist my hand in the opposite direction, seeking her sweet heat. Cece's hips rise on contact. She slides her hand under the waistband of my pants and grips my hard cock. I tug the fabric to my thighs cause I'm helpful like that and it'll put Cees right where I want her faster.

My palms rest on her hips and her delicate fingers line me up. She gets a pretty pink blush in her cheeks before impaling herself on my shaft.

I flex up, deep and fast.

"Oh fuck, Dusty!" She screams at the swift intrusion.

Dear God, I could listen to that noise over and over and never be sick of knowing I'm the one about to make her come.

If this is the last time before we head back to Brighton, I want it hard and rough with Cece panting, choking out my name as she drenches my balls. A week from now, I'll lay her down and take her slow, the way I've been able to the past forty-eight hours. Until then, we're both going to remember how amazing being together feels.

The tension in her body eases as her pussy adjusts to my size. I feel every inch of her and she does me. Our tongues tangle, nipping and biting. Loving on one another the way we've learn to do best, but with the added power awakened this weekend by sleeping in the same bed and sharing parts of ourselves in more than a biblical manner.

I cup her lush ass, grinding her clit against the base of my cock. Surrounded by the knowledge that what few parts of herself this woman hasn't given me, she'll surrender before long.

I'm lost in her big brown eyes, staring at me in wonder. So much so, the snick of the front lock after being picked is inaudible. The slam of the door as the knob crashes through the drywall, Morgan's crazed expression in the threshold, and the pistol he's got in his solid grip, however, are hard to ignore.

"Fucking hell!" I bark, startled, and pull Cece to my chest.

The blinding light refracting off of the snow has us squinting.

"Jesus Christ, what are you doing here!" Cece screams, her attention on the open threshold.

I reach over us for a quilt that's covering the back of the couch.

"What am I doing? What are you doing!" Morgan yells from the open space. His brotherly voice reminds me of two kids in the thralls of a pissing match.

"What the hell? I can't unsee this, Cece." Morgan groans.

"Well, it's not as if you're trying! Look away, you idiot!" She screeches. "Could you at least have the decency to wait outside so we can find our clothes?"

Morgan's intense, red cheeks fill with air. He's a balloon about to pop. I owe him an explanation, but I'm not giving it with my pants around my ankles. Not when he's gotten an eye full of Cece and me going at it.

He walks out, leaving the door wide open. Cece and I untangle our limbs and gooseflesh appears on my skin.

She rushes for the bedroom to find clothes to put on and comes back out in those grey sweatpants. Hopping on one foot, Cece manages to get a second wooly sock on before venturing out in the cold. "I'm sorry. I'll be right back." Overwhelmed our romantic weekend has taken a downturn, she forgets her boots.

It's bright out in the yard. Cees uses her hand as a visor coming down the steps. Her brother's barking into his cell that he's found her.

I follow her lead, tossing my drawstring pants covered in her pussy juice in the hamper and snatching something to wear from my dresser drawer that doesn't advertise we've been fucking all weekend. Not that Morgan hasn't figured it out, but yeah... respect. My best guess is he issued an Amber alert for his sister and assembled the troops.

"How did you know I was here?" Cece is saying as I get back to the front door. The cold from the frozen ground has begun seeping into her feet and she rotates lifting them as her toes go numb.

"Nobody could get ahold of you. Skye and I went through a week's worth of surveillance tape at the mill and the only thing off was you getting out of Dusty's truck. You were fighting and then this weekend you both disappear. The last location your cell pinged off of was nearby."

"Then what made you feel like it was okay to burst in with a gun?"

Christ, where did he even get a gun? As a felon, Morgan can get sent back to jail for possessing one.

"He was acting suspicious. You were fighting on the tape. Both of your phones were off and I had no way of telling if you came of your own free will!" He pegs her with a frigid stare.

"I forgot my charger." Cees wrings her stinging hands. "And my battery died. I didn't think anything of it."

Morgan doesn't believe his sister at all. I'm pissed at his stupid ass for the attempted rescue. But I'm choking down the line Celine's fed me. Her cell dying aside, her intentions weren't as innocuous as she's making them out to be.

I don't know what she was supposed to do different, but I was a fool not to ask who knew she was coming to Boone with me. Women nowadays text their best friends every damn thing from their Tinder swipe right's profile information to the dick pic he private messages before they hook up. They call it safety. But a decent amount is bullshit bragging.

Now that the blinder's ripped off, I'm flashing back the flawless coincidence I could arrive early at the medical park on Friday and to Cece's high-heeled jog across the street when we agreed I'd pick her up at the mill for our date.

It doesn't matter how different it would be if I could go back to the beginning and do things right. I'm Celine's dirty little secret.

"You didn't tell anyone where you were going. How was I to know he wasn't forcing you—" Morgan cracks his knuckles.

"I'm fine." She plants her hands under her pits, searching for some body heat.

"Obvious now, Celine." Cece's brother grits out like it's a little too late. He's also not interested in discussing what he walked in on.

Not that I want to either, so I stay silent, letting the anger build.

"Then I guess I'm on my way." Morgan's jaw ticks, his ire is directed at Celine. Yet, his full attention is on me.

Not that I give a rat's ass what Morgan thinks of walking in on his sister while she's got her legs spread. At this moment, I hate them both.

Chapter Twenty-one

Celine

What happened is on me, and I owe everyone an apology for making them worry. It's my priority when we get back to Brighton. Right now, all I want is a chance to make it right with Dusty. The "sorry" I gave him while rushing out of the house wasn't close to enough to cover how badly I've blown it. I want to hug him and explain away his fears. The ones I had a few days ago have ruined everything. The least I can do is be honest and hope he can forgive me.

I spin to dash up the stairs. Dusty fills the gap in the doorway. In the few minutes it's taken to talk Morgan down, he's put on jeans and a soft henley. Like most shirts, it binds over his biceps.

I try not to lose it seeing his sharp scowl. What Dusty says next pierces my heart. But it's warranted, and I'm certain the pang in my chest isn't cutting as deep as the wounds he carries.

"Go."

"What?" I blink fast and shake my head, thinking I haven't heard Dusty correctly. I haven't combed my hair and the messy knots from my bedhead pull, pinching my scalp.

"GET OUT!" His voice booms into the rafters, shaking the house. Dusty could blow it down with his breath. His muscles clench and anger radiates from his body. "Whatever we're doing, it's over. I'm done with the game of pretend."

"I wasn't—This weekend."

"This weekend means nothing." Dusty towers over me.

My neck cranes and my head tips back all the way, trying not to show any intimidation, but for the first time I don't feel safe with him. He's scaring me.

He clenches his fists at his side, holding back his anger. It's as if it's taking every ounce of control not to grab me by the arms and shake some sense into me. I've never taken him as a violent man, but I've bested his temper. I pushed him so far he's holding back the beast that he hates people believing he is.

I want to tell him, *"This weekend was perfect. It was what I expected I'd have a million years from now. You're the kind of man who I thought was waiting in the wings. I was blind not to see you've been there all along."* But none of those words leave my mouth because it's too late.

My shoulders slump in resignation. This is all my fault. Dusty lets me past him into the house only enough to snag my purse off the counter. I run to catch Morgan. He's backed out, but I'm able to flag him down before he puts the car in drive.

A mile down the road, my brother pulls into a gas station.

"You want anything?" He notices my shiver when he opens the door and tosses me a sweatshirt. I have no shoes or coat, and it's more than I deserve.

"No." I stare out the window.

Morgan fills up at the pump and we drive all the way back to Brighton, unspeaking. The clear blue sky near the mountains gives way to dark rain clouds as we cross the state. The barometer falls putting pressure on my ears that seeps into my bones crushing me from the outside in. Overwhelmed, I'm helpless to stop the tears tumbling down my cheeks. My blotchy and swollen face seems to gloat back at me in the side mirror, proving how wrong I was. I stop worrying Morgan will notice and use the sleeves of his sweatshirt as a tissue. I can't slide any further down the ladder of embarrassment than I have, and I can't pity myself for the problems I've caused everyone else.

Morgan shifts his SUV into park. We stare at the brick and green trimmed factory windows.

"I don't get it, Cece. It's not as if we don't know him. You can't even buck up the courage to say he'd invited you to Boone as friends. And you let me drive all the way up there under the impression he was hurting you. That the guy we've all trusted wasn't as trustworthy as we'd believed, when it was you who lied."

"I wasn't lying."

"Do you hear yourself? Sloan, Kimber, Aidy? None of your friends knew where you were! Women tell their fucking girlfriends everything. But you disappear without a goddamn word to anyone. With the shifty way he's acted when it comes to you, how could I *not* be worried?"

"You pulled a gun on us! You and these people— whoever they are, whatever you're involved with— they've made you comfortable enough to barge into a house ready to shoot!"

"These people? You set me up with these people! What did you expect, fucking cucumber finger sandwiches and four o'clock tea?"

"I didn't ask you to come after me! After Dusty!"

"You owe me an explanation. One I can give to Carver, so you'd better not leave a fricken' thing out." Morgan stops yelling at me.

Humid air fogs the windows. I want to draw pictures on them the way we had as kids and we were too innocent to see what was going on around us.

"Are you even willing to admit how long you've been seeing Dusty?"

"A while," I bite my lip. "This was the first chance we had to go be alone together. I didn't let on because what if it didn't work out?" I'd even convinced myself that unless I stuck to my plan, I'd wind up like Mom or Amy.

What I hadn't told Dusty, but Morgan knows is Amy was my very best friend. Her boyfriend skipped out once she'd paid his bail, leaving her to raise their child alone. Amy's method of staying afloat became finding another man and having another baby, starting the cycle all over again. That kind of influence from the women I was closest to was an affliction in themselves.

"Mom got bogged down with a baby on her hip and one in her belly, watching her dreams get flushed down the toilet. And then giving up when drugs provided an easy out."

"But she started using when we were older."

"There are things you don't know about Mom and Dad." Many times it got worse when Morgan went out of town for games or got camp scholarships that took him away for what felt like weeks on end.

Morgan's palm flips in a gesture as if to say, "like what?"

"He hit her Morgan. I don't know when it started, but I found out right after Amy's boyfriend went to jail for beating her up. I walked into the kitchen to put back the bandages I'd taken with me to Amy's. It was obvious Mom was high. She'd been rifling through the cabinets and turned after snatching them from the shelf with a shiner on her eye."

"How can you be so certain it was Dad?"

"After everything, why do you still give him credit?

Look at the past ten years; he dropped you like a hot potato when you became better at basketball than he'd been. He told everyone when you went to jail it was just desserts for you bragging about getting a scholarship. Mom and Dad only latched on when it made them look good or when they needed something. She called me to see if I'd write her a prescription, Morgan. She broke her arm and even after it's healing she wants pain relief."

"Oxy?"

I nod my head and my brother blows a long hard breath. Our parents faked it until we'd grown up enough where they couldn't pull the wool over our eyes anymore.

"Dad did it?" I hear him lose the last bit of hope he held onto.

Having lousy parents fills you with dread. There's always this tiny storm cloud ready to overshadow any happiness and remind you a bit of the same darkness resides inside your heart. Because of this, there's a little part of both of us desperate to believe we weren't as bad off as we were.

I want Mom's love the way Morgan wants Dad's approval. I needed my mother to tell me she was proud of my accomplishments, not the crushing blow when my usefulness was tied to what I could do for her.

"Mom is an addict and Dad's hurt her before. It could have gone a million ways. Reading into whether or not Mom had an accident is fruitless. She lies to cover up the truth. Besides, we agreed a long time ago some people don't want help. Their choices are too ingrained." I have no remorse for keeping this particular secret from him.

Morgan lets another layer of reality sink down into the abyss we left behind when we became adults. Dad had roughed Morgan up a few times, but not enough to leave visible marks. Our father had encouraged

Morgan's basketball skills. So when my brother's sportsmanship gained him a way out, the emotional scars our father's jealousy left on him endured.

I'd rather love nobody at all than for a child of mine to wind up surrounded by people who don't care.

"There's something else." I've rubbed my snotty face on my brother's sweatshirt so many times I have rug burn under my nose. I have no dignity left to lose, so I might as well hammer the last nails into my coffin.

"What?" Morgan studies me with genuine concern.

Blowing out a deep breath pushes more tears to the surface and sure my stomach. "I was afraid I'd have to defend him."

"Who, Dusty?" Morgan stuffs his fingers in his eye sockets. "Hate to break it to you, Cece, the guy's built like a brick shithouse. Unless..." It dawns on him. "Wow. I'm speechless. I mean, I'm not sure I'm proud of you for admitting a human reaction, or it makes me angrier because the sister I grew up with wasn't—"

"Judgemental? Self-conscious?"

"The first one, no. The second part I always thought you had under control better than the rest of us."

"I didn't know what people were going to say. I didn't want to hear anyone talk down about him and not be able to explain he wasn't stupid. Or be teased about why I was with him." I didn't even understand our attraction.

"By us? Awesome, Cece. We're your friends." He inhales through his nose. "Glad you think so highly of us." He mutters "dumbass" toward the driver's window. "Okay, pretend I'm bashing one of my best friends because he takes a bit longer to speak and when he does it's with a stutter. I've got one better!" Morgan holds up a finger in challenge. "Explain to me why you're shacked up in the woods with this hulking, perpetually pissed off stalker guy, who has spent the past year glowering at you while you take your clothes off, chases after you with a permanent boner, and stammers to get out ev-er-y sen-tence." Morgan mimics Dusty's speech patterns.

My palm flattens and I do something I've never done. I slap my brother hard across the cheek.

"Oh, God!" I cover my mouth, ashamed. "I shouldn't have hit you. See, I can't be with Dusty. He has a daughter. What if I'm like Mom and Dad? I can't bring this on them. He's got the biggest heart and all he's trying to do is raise his little girl. She means everything to him. He's not so damn cocky that he's beneath playing tea party and knows every princess name well enough to tease her by mixing them up. They ski and they're already their own tiny family. Even if I'm not ready for kids now, he's exactly the type of father I wanted my children to have because his kindness would make up for everything awful inside of me." I shake my head since none of those things are meant for me. I should be alone so I can't hurt anyone the way I did Dusty today, become an addict like my mother, or lay a hand on people the way my father has.

My brother looks at me with utter disbelief. "Fuck, I've never seen you stand up for anyone before like this, Cece." He rubs his cheek. "You're falling in love with Dusty."

"How long does it take to fall out of love?" I whisper, crestfallen. Dusty's feelings for me changed on a dime. I won't be so fortunate.

"I don't know, sis. It's not the same and we might not see Mom and Dad, but the kid I was hasn't managed to stop loving the parents he thought he had. After reality sets in, I guess there are always people who you still hold out hope for?

"I can tell you one thing, for all the times I got in his face over you, Dusty's held his ground. The man's a stone wall that doesn't budge. He's not the type to need anyone to go on a tirade and defend him. And," Morgan continues with regret, "he probably would've had a second princess on his arm if I hadn't been an overbearing jerk."

Chapter Twenty-two

Celine

My brother promises not to disown me and drives off, heading for home. I dodge puddles on my way into the building and slink up the stairs close to the drywall, hoping no one sees me.

Still hoping no one sees me. What a laugh. I keep hiding and getting caught hasn't taught me much, has it? I'm a wreck and the only person to blame is myself. Yet, I still want time to compose myself and figure out how to explain.

I move the red velvet rope when my feet hit the landing at the third floor, inch to the side, and reattach it to the brass hook on the wall.

My door is open and light coming through the window casts a dreary pattern on the hallway floor. I pass by noticing my lamp is on and Sloan's perched cross-legged on my bed.

She jumps up, a mix of relief and concern etched her features. "Where have you been!" The accusatory questions only one of your best friends has the right to ask follow rapid-fire from behind me about Boone,

Dusty, and how I could've taken off without confiding in her.

I've been in the car for so long I don't think twice about my destination until I'm pushing into the bathroom. The sight of the tranquil sage decor sets me off. About to piss myself, I have to instruct my bladder to hold on.

Covering my mouth, a racked sob escapes. It's so loud and degrading and I lose what little composure I've got left. Not only have I given all the people who love me the illusion I don't trust them, I've also left them with the impression Dusty isn't trustworthy. What's worse is because of my insecurities, I have blown it with the nicest guy I'll ever meet.

After our date, Dusty gave me a second chance. What did my brother see on the security camera feed that made him incite a posse and drive fricken' halfway across the state? Obviously, a woman who hesitated to get too close while arguing with a man twice her size. I had to have looked frightened by what Dusty wanted from me...because I was. It's not as if Dusty hadn't made me aware Morgan was out for him either. If something happened to me, he'd be the first logical suspect. By taking off, I'd done nothing to ease anyone's concerns.

Until this weekend, I'd been so damn scared to get in over my head with a man. I stood at the edge of the wood, facing the wrong direction. It's stupid to lament I couldn't see the forest for the trees. But when it comes down to it? If I'd simply turned around, shifted my perspective, Dusty had been standing in the clearing.

I'd wanted the perfect romance with the perfect timing. But considering my flawed home life, what did I know of any of that? My unwillingness to accept imperfections—in my plan and in the man I've harbored feelings for—leaves me in no better situation than I've avoided.

I'd asked him to hold me to a higher standard and can't beg him to change his mind. There's no way Dusty will trust me after this and no chance we'll ever be a couple now. Those stupid images of us I'd entertained as I came to my senses are flushed down the toilet.

Sloan's waiting when I finish in the stall. I wash my hands. She offers me a towel and then a tissue for my uncontrollable waterworks.

Sympathy laced, yet in true girlfriend fashion, she doesn't mince words. "You look like hell. Want to talk about it?"

I let out a ragged breath, trying to stop from feeling sorry for myself anymore. It's futile when my mind draws a silly parallel: my tears are like a burst pipe and the handyman isn't here to patch it up. Why, when I've acted so ashamed of Dusty, should I expect he'd fix me? I mean, I was proving I was capable of turning my shitty life into something I could be proud of, wasn't I?

Of all the times I was my own cheerleader, I'm not proud anymore. I'm the worst kind of person. My education didn't better me. I'm as led by the preconceived notions and worry about the judgments of others as anyone.

"Okay, I'll start." She puts her hand on her hips, downloading everything that's gone on here during my absence. "The sublet deal on the condo near Holly fell through. She'd tried to get in touch a bunch of times so you could go see it. When that didn't work, she messaged the group chat. Nobody could find hide nor hair of you and the boys went nuts. They were down in the offices, going through the tape, and finding your last GPS coordinates. Morgan took off before Carver had a chance to tell him he'd called Renata. It didn't make a difference to Morgan. In his mind, you needed rescuing. So we all—Aidy included, and my advice is you might want to buck up and kiss her ass for making her worry about you *and* Morgan—have been waiting on pins and needles.

"Even after they figured out where you were, I'm still shaking over the idea something awful happened. I can't deal with the 'what ifs', Cece. What if you'd *actually* been abducted by an *actual* stranger? We love you so much. How were we ever supposed to get over that? Now, you're back. So why don't you fill in the blanks?"

"We left on Friday. I wanted to figure out how I felt about Dusty. And, in the end, I proved I was exactly what I feared I was to him."

"Which is?"

"His cum dumpster."

"Ooooh, Honey! I'm not even sure what that means other than to tell you we are not using those words. Not now. Not ever."

"It means—"

"I get the drift! But you are so much more. He wouldn't have taken you away for the weekend if all he wanted was to get you into bed. I'm guessing you were already sleeping together?"

"Not in a bed." I criticize myself.

"Okay in the cab of his truck, the dressing room at Sweet Caroline's." Sloan rattles off places she assumes Dusty and I were having sex based on the camera footage the guys pulled when I was missing.

Geez, once the cat's out of the bag everyone cozies up with popcorn to watch the shitshow your life's become.

"The ladies' room," I apologize because the remorse I've had for breaking the rule has lingered for forever.

"Ew, at the club?"

I worry my lip and look at the tile under my feet.

"*THIS* bathroom?"

The silence between us lets a horrified Sloan draw her own conclusions. "Are you done in here?"

I swallow, presuming she means using the facilities.

Although I've been doing a lot more in here, haven't I? When I don't answer Sloan drags me by the hand to my room. I fully expect she'll throw a suitcase on the bed. Instead, she pulls the covers down.

"Lie down."

My jaw drops.

"Do you need me to tell you that you're a bitch? You are. Cece. You're a total cunt. I'm pissed at you, but I'm still here. Now get comfy and don't leave out a damn detail." She flops against the pillows, expecting me to do the same.

I slide down, lying on a bed which doesn't feel like my own anymore. Sloan does too. We're face to face. She uses her thumbs to wipe the teardrops from underneath my eyes.

"Ladies room aside, how bad did you fuck up?"

"The most important people in my life hate me."

"No, they don't. For as worried as I was and mad as I am, not me. And Morgan overreacted because he loves you, Hon. His jail time was rough. I've seen how protective of you he's been since he got out. It's as if he's trying to make up for leaving you with no one. Count your lucky stars, if you haven't noticed, he's ten times worse when it comes to Aidy." Sloan's brow creases and she frowns.

Sloan's got a messed up past of her own. While mine pales in comparison, she knows it lacks the warm fuzzies. I spill the parts I've told my brother and give Sloan the extra details he's unlikely to appreciate.

"I thought I was some dumb stripper everyone wanted to fuck. So when he didn't ask me out, how was I supposed to know Dusty wanted a relationship? It was rotten. I loved being with him and still hated how cheap what we were doing and lying about it made me feel."

I leave out how I hadn't wanted the girls to taunt me. Given my reaction, slapping Morgan, I'm sure I would have defended Dusty to anyone in a heartbeat and made them regret their disbelief that this man made me happy. I'd likely have bitten back to a lewd comment about Dusty's anatomy with one of my own. The kind that, no matter the size, would make them wonder if their man *measured up*.

When it comes down to it and I had a chance to explain, I would tell Dusty. After the way my actions wounded his pride, he deserves undistilled honesty. This is something we won't come back from, and he needs to understand how much I regret it.

"It was easier to make you the bad guys when it was me." I do admit to Sloan. "If there was a reason to second guess anything, I did. I let my miserable past lead me into a miserable future so I didn't get stuck giving up on PA school."

"Did Dusty ever ask you to give up on what you wanted?"

"No, I never even gave him a chance to get that far. But you were right when you said he was serious about us if he was introducing me to his daughter. He was in a rush to bring us all up there together." Not as if it matters now.

"What did you say?"

"We should go slower. She's a sweet girl, but I'm not ready to be a mother. I didn't have the best role model." I don't doubt for a minute I'd get attached to Sylvie. But going from cum du—the word we're not using anymore —to girlfriend to second mommy in a week is too much. I'm understanding how rigid my plan was. It didn't give me any flexibility for someone as wonderful as Dusty to come into my life. However, I can't throw it all out the window to fit the mold of someone else's dreams.

"At least you were willing to compromise something." Her nose bunches and her mouth twists as if to reinforce my plan was awfully rigid for her taste.

My shoulder gets stuck on the mattress as they shrug

and my lip wobbles. "I really began to think Dusty and I were changing things between us for the better. Starting something new. I was going to tell you where I'd been when he dropped me off. I swear, Sloan."

In actuality, I couldn't wait to tell her. Hollowness has replaced my excitement from a few hours ago. It's my fault for not letting anyone in until it was too late. You can kill people with kindness and still keep a wall around your heart.

Chapter Twenty-three

Holly steps out of the townhouse with a tiny fenced-in backyard she shares with her sister.

It's unseasonably warm for late winter. The sheen of sweat on my skin is a nice change, but I'll be happy when it cools off tomorrow.

The three kids are playing kickball and tormenting us with requests to set up the sprinkler so they can run through it. Putting aside the few grumbles when I remind her she has no bathing suit, Sylvie's having a blast.

Holly and Laurel invited Sylvie and me over for the afternoon while Renata's away. The burgers Laurel is flipping are repayment for having Bhodi over a while back. I have guilt my mother-in-law is missing out, but on those "how would you rate your pain" scales that go from grinning to crying, it's a notch up from the anger and resentment I've harbored over other things.

Holly pushes a beer into my hand and sits next to me on the wooden steps.

"Thanks."

"Meh, you looked as if you needed one."

"It shows?"

"Every time you try not to talk about her."

Pissed as hell, I slammed shit around, packing up my stuff almost as soon as Cece ran down the driveway and hauling my fuming ass up the highway. Irate, I'd let her cast a dark cloud over my spot in the woods where I'm starting over. It cost me more than a broken heart. A trooper pulled me over outside of Greensboro. Being a hulking man with speech problems is difficult on the best of days, topped off with my obvious anger? Yeah, it went over like a lead balloon, adding an hour onto the trek home.

Finally back from Boone, Renata didn't hold back asking how it went. After dealing with the police, I was curt telling her we hadn't seen eye to eye on a few things. Leaving out, namely, Cece hadn't any desire for a relationship with a man like me.

Celine having me pick her up from the medical park seems obvious now. The only way I'd begun to believe she took off without telling anyone is how fast she snagged her purse and turned tail. Not that I wanted her back inside. She ruined fucking everything.

I've got the rest of her stuff shoved in a garbage bag in the back of the truck. This is my week off while Renata is away. I took vacation since she's soaking up the sunshine on the swabbed deck of a cruise liner. Sylvie's booster is in the cab again, and she was quick to tell me it smelled like the lady in the red dress. I'm glad she forgot her name. I'd like to forget it too.

I finally understand Celine's ashamed of me. Of everything we've shared. I'm the man who gets her off, not even worth mentioning in passing.

What kind of idiot was I introducing my daughter to her? I'm not even certain where the seed of faith we'd all mesh came from. Maybe I'm a fucking lonely loser. Or as big a moron as people try making me out to be.

Now I'm grateful for Renata's comments about things progressing too fast as much as I hate having ignored her warnings.

I haven't had much to distract me in between school drop-off and pick-up, princess movies, and tucking Sylvie in after a bedtime story. I've dissected my life reading the pages of princess pop-up books, and in this fairytale nobody saw past the frog's warts.

Holly got an earful of gossip at the club already, so I've spilled few details about the disastrous weekend. She also admitted she had a sense something was up between me and Celine, but where we'd been tight-lipped about it, she hadn't wanted to bring it up.

I grip my chin. "How'd you figure out it was her?"

"You mean, beyond the fact that the vein in your neck bulged during every one of her performances? I thought it was weird she smelled like you. Then you wandered over to the bar and smelled like her."

"You sniffed it out over the club's stale sweat and alcohol stench?"

Seriously? Do women have some sort of scent super-power no one's informed me of? I'm unprepared if this is a talk I'm going to have to have with my daughter along with the birds and the bees.

"The sniffer never fails." Holly twitches her nose a la *Bewitched* reruns. I swear had I listened hard enough there would have been the tinkling sound.

"It does too," Laurel pronounces. "You have an ex-asshole no different from the rest of us."

Holly ignores her sister's comment. "I told you, Big Guy." Holly leans her head on my arm. "Don't date strippers, the waitstaff or co-workers of any kind. Don't date soldiers or anyone in the military either."

"Doesn't leave many choices." Laurel twirls a pair of barbecue tongs in her hand. "If your list of acceptable partners gets any shorter, your lady parts are going to shrivel up."

"My vagina is happy on its own, fuck you very much." Holly tosses her sister the middle finger.

"Y'all should date each other." Laurel points the tongs back-and-forth.

Holly and I make room for the Holy Spirit and a dozen of his favorite saints, regarding each other with undisguised revulsion. Hey, at least we both have the same gut reaction.

Holly follows it up with, "Dusty's too young for me, anyhow." Our true feelings aired, she scoots back and throws an arm around me. "He should be with someone equally as sexy, though."

"As sexy as me or you?" My chest rumbles.

"Uh, me?" She uses the 'duh' tone.

"So, Dusty, include nobody older or younger to your list too. That way your man parts can shrivel up alongside Holly's girlie ones. I still say it would work between you two. The kids get along great and we wouldn't have to worry about repair bills."

I've fixed a few things here and there for Laurel. If I charged her for more than the parts, it would be in char-grilled meats. Laurel makes a mean burger. "Something broken?"

"Nope. It would just be convenient." Laurel's admission makes me laugh and we wind up joking around about some of my worst repair calls. Before Laurel heads inside to get a platter, a part of me almost forgets how we got on the subject to begin with.

Then Holly looks me in the eyes and it's all back. I see how hard it is for her to be alone too. "You really liked her, huh, Dust?"

I scrub my face. "Yeah... I did."

"Not no more?" she confirms with a sad smile, rubbing my bicep.

I shake my head once and look between my boots planted on the step below. Celine's demand I hold her to a higher standard came back to bite her in the butt.

I'm not wasting any more time with a woman like her. I'm not even thirty, and this life's taken too much of a toll on me. I don't have more to give people who can't appreciate me.

"I still can't believe you're tossing up quitting. It'll be weird without you around at Sweet Caroline's."

The same as when I opted to hand in my notice at the engineering firm, it's been a chore not to ruminate over everyone's reactions.

"Nothing good will come from me going back to work at the mill whether Celine Wescott lives there or not."

Holly forces a weak smile. "I wish this wasn't happening to you."

"Thanks."

"I've got a little more bad news, though. My neighbor three doors down is moving to India for a year. He leased his apartment to Cece on Monday and she moves in early next month."

It's like a shot in the solar plexus, but I'd wanted a clean break, didn't I? I chug down the last of my beer and Laurel offloads a second into my paw. Her expression matches the one Holly had a moment ago. The whiny old forty-five lyrics about breaking it to me gently gets stuck on repeat between my ears as I realize why Laurel had gone inside.

I clink the bottle's neck to the one Laurel's opened for herself. "Bring your tongs next time. We'll barbecue at Renata's." Cause I won't be back here again until Cece is gone.

Sylvie clings to my neck as I carry her up the squeaky wooden staircase at the factory. In the living area, I set her down on one of the comfy couches, leaving the sack of Celine's shit hidden behind it.

"You'll be fine here." I pull my cell out of my pocket. Unlocking it, I touch the folder with age-appropriate apps.

"Kay, Daddy." Clearing her throat, my daughter hugs a stuffed snowman she's been using as a pillow most of today and places the phone on a sofa cushion. She's disinterested in the streaming preschool show I chose to keep her distracted while I take care of business.

Sylvie came down with a runny nose overnight. I kept her home from school and gave her medicine when all the snuffing led to a headache. She hasn't wanted to eat or drink much, but that's every kindergartener, right?

Holly's on tonight and where Sylvie's not feeling well anyhow, I don't want to drop her with Laurel and pass anything along. At least if she encounters any adults, they're more apt to soap up. I would be, anyway.

We've got to meet Renata's plane after this and I need to be able to tell my mother-in-law I'm looking for a new job without her offering unsolicited advice on ditching my old one. For as open as my relationship with Renata is, she's unaware of what goes behind the scenes here. I need to wash my hands of the mill now. I've already tempted fate. The last thing I want to explain to Renata is how fast everything in Boone went down the drain.

Carver and everyone else have been blowing up my phone all week. I ignored the texts and voice messages until someone put Sloan into the mix. Only then did I respond with a simple **on vacation**. Until I'd made my decision and agreed to meet, there wasn't anything to say.

"Be back. In there, if you need me." I toss a thumb toward Carver's suite.

Her chin wrinkles, but doesn't tremble. I reassure her she's my brave girl, that this won't take more than ten minutes tops, and watch as she rests her eyes the way she had on the trek through Brighton to get here.

I rap on the door to Carver's suite and leave it cracked when he has me enter. I've done a bunch of repairs in the private space. While his living room has an expanse of windows, it's decorated warmer, cozy and informal in opposition to the stark white of the common area I've left my daughter in. However, today the number of people here gives the impression I'm meeting the fucking inquisition when stepping inside. The three main stakeholders sit on a plush couch like a tribunal.

Trig silently nods at me. He and Jake flank either side of Carver. Morgan's holding up the far wall with one leg tented and the opposite foot pressed against the brick. His arms are crossed.

"This is stupid," I mutter, tossing the keyring that allows me access to everything here and at Sweet Caroline's on a side table.

"Listen, Dusty, we're truly sorry about what happened," Carver speaks.

"Great. Thanks. I quit."

"You can't fucking quit on me!" Jake's the first to get defensive and I love how he's made it about himself. So much so, it's no problem forming the words to call him an asshole.

"Celine took responsibility. There's no need to turn in your notice." Carver pretends to be the voice of reason.

"He came into my house with a gun," I state firmly, pointing at Morgan.

"I didn't know!" he interrupts. Carver glares at Morgan as if his presence was only allowed on the condition he was seen and not heard.

I peg him with a hard glare. "My kid could have been

there. Wh-at then, Morgan? You were so goddamn amped up believing I was holding your sister against her will. What if Cece wasn't even there? What if you pulled a gun on my daughter? What if you shot first and asked questions later?"

"I'm sorry. Everything—*my past*—it got the best of me. I was worried about Cece the way I worry about Aidy."

"You're not the only man in this room with demons. Not the only one trying to keep anyone safe."

"You gotta trust me," he pleads.

"Why? Where did all the trust you had in me evaporate to?" Mine in Morgan flew out the door when he barged in, entitled. This is the same friend who asked me to safeguard his sister. How had his request for me to walk Celine home one night turned into this line of suspicion?

"If the two of you had told us sooner," Carver interjects, steepling his hands. "And I'm not saying adults aren't entitled to privacy. It was a huge misunderstanding. We can get past it."

"Not in-terested."

"Stay on at the club. I'll give you a raise," Jake blurts.

"Fuck off." I turn my back on the four.

Chapter Twenty-four

The men I've broken ties with squawk like goddamn chickens as I step out of Carver's apartment. I'd been upfront the first time Carver handed out a "Christmas Bonus" I wasn't interested in delving into their underworld. I'm not one of Carver's flunkies. I don't take orders from Trig the way Morgan does. My job around here was to fix things.

My appreciation for Carver's help ended when Morgan busted the lock on my cabin door. How the hell am I supposed to have faith in them that things won't get worse if they haven't any in me?

When it comes down to it, I've earned a fair wage being at their beck and call. Everything I've done has been on the up and up. They don't need me to snake a drain when there's someone a lot more qualified to do it cheaper. And there's no reason to worry I'll rat them out to the cops. There are too many good women who'd get hurt.

My only desire is washing my hands of it all. The mill is one less complication in my already complicated life.

The door snicks closed behind me, muffling the noise the cocksuckers are making. I swear those pricks are yelling as much at one another as they are for me to come back. "No" isn't an answer they're keen on hearing, but my attention lands on a bigger problem.

Sylvie's stretched out on the couch and Cece is sitting on the middle cushion talking in a hushed tone to her. I'm about to stomp over, snatch up my child, and head for the hills when I watch Cece's palm cover Sylvie's forehead. An expression halfway between anguish and resignation crosses my daughter's face.

"You're warm, Sylvie Rhys. You said you have a headache?"

"All day." My little girl clears her throat again. It hasn't been constant, but has happened enough now I'm noticing.

"What about a tickle in your throat? Is it scratchy?"

Sylvie swallows with the same hesitancy as she does eating Brussel sprouts.

"Daddy's giving me more medicine before we get Grandma." She turns her head toward me like the children's dose of acetaminophen I'm set to give her with dinner will make all her worries go away.

Mine? They've skyrocketed. And not because this is my first time seeing Celine since she bolted from Boone.

Cece faces me.

"Your stuff's over there." I point behind the couch, my tone and mannerisms gruff.

"Can I talk to your daddy for a minute, Sylvie Rhys?"

"Uh, huh," she mumbles with no fight.

Celine approaches me like I'm a viper. My jaw ticks and my muscles tense. I word vomit a sentence or two about how Sylvie's been under the weather today, repeating I've dropped off Cece's stuff. She doesn't pay any heed to her bags, asking about my child.

"When did her symptoms start?"

"This morning. Listen, we're going to be late to get Renata." We're not. Done here, there's zero reasons to stay.

"What's she been taking?"

I shake my head, indulging her medical curiosity more because I'm not interested in causing a scene with Sylvie as a witness. "Rotating acetaminophen and ibuprofen." The way Renata taught me to.

"And her last dose was a few hours ago?"

"Yes." I blow out a breath, not happy with the interrogation.

"Dusty, she's really warm. I bet if I ran to get a thermometer it's over a hundred degrees. Uncontrolled by the fever reducers you're using, that makes me concerned."

We both look over and Sylvie shivers. I notice a slight sheen of sweat at her temple.

"I know we're not on the best of terms, but would you mind—"

I scoff, interrupting.

"For everyone's sake, I'd feel better assessing what's wrong with Sylvie, but I won't overstep. I don't want you to leave without knowing if what she has might be more."

"What do you think it is?" Arms crossed, I'm stoic.

"I mean, it could be as simple as a bug she picked up at school. But, for some kids, strep presents with a high fever that's not easily brought down to normal with over-the-counter meds. She'd need antibiotics."

I'm ready to tell Cece "whatever". I'll get Sylvie an appointment at the pediatrician's tomorrow. My daughter can see the doctor and he'll take care of it. I don't want Celine Wescott treating my kid out of some sense of guilt. I'd have rather not seen her again at all. But she also works at the pediatric office Sylvie goes to, and with my luck, we'll wind up running into her all over again, ruining another day.

Sylvie sneezes, coughs, and croaks. When she looks over at me with watery eyes like she's certain I can cure anything that ails her, it changes my mind and I agree to let Celine examine her.

She's got to go get a thermometer. By the time she's returning, the other guys are filtering out of Carver's apartment. I scowl for them to keep their opinions to themselves while waiting on the instrument's final verdict.

Jake bolts. Morgan stays put, protective of his sister and ramping up my desire to throat punch the bastard. As if he and I haven't had words not ten minutes ago. Trig's telling some story about Owen's last big cold to fill the silence.

Cece frowns, looking at the digital readout when the thermometer beeps. "One hundred and two point six. How high was it with her first dose this morning?"

"One-o-one."

"Has it gotten back to normal?"

"Close. Once."

Cece pulls a tongue depressor from her blouse pocket. "Can you open up for me, Sylvie?"

My daughter obliges and they wince in unison. Celine makes Morgan go get Sylvie a drink from the kitchen.

"Water?"

"Ginger ale, if Dad is okay with soda. Her throat is extremely raw, Dusty. I'm suggesting you take her for a rapid strep tonight at the children's emergency room."

I allow Morgan to get Sylvie the sweeter drink so she's not swallowing shards of glass. She needs fluids and I'm dancing the single-dad fine line. I promised Renata we'd be at the airport and Sylvie needs to go to the doctor.

"I'll pick up Renata." Cece offers when I hedge, unable to take her immediate suggestion. Morgan and Trig offer to bail me out too, but I firmly decline. The barrel I'm over sucks and Celine's the lesser of the evils. At least Renata and she have met. The redness seeping from Celine's collar also means she's not interested in rehashing what went wrong between us with my mother-in-law.

I whip off a text for Renata to find when she lands and boots her cell, and write down the flight info for Celine.

The out-of-body experience trying to coordinate madness while things are going wrong has my head pounding on the way to the ER. It adds to the parental guilt over missing the signs and underestimating how sick my daughter is. With a migraine coming on, I can't imagine how Sylvie's felt all day.

Buckled into her booster, Sylvie tells me her belly hurts and things go from bad to worse. Taking glances in the rearview, I reassure her we'll be at the hospital soon. The silver lining is she doesn't puke in the truck. Ghost white with a green tinge, a nurse behind the partition in reception takes one look at Sylvie and makes me the responsible party for a pink plastic bedpan. We're ushered to a room before I've got her insurance card back in my wallet.

And then someone's pressed the pause button again and we wait, stuck in a little four by four windowless cage. Eventually, a nurse comes in to get Sylvie's vitals, a doctor who orders tests, and the same nurse swabs Sylvie's throat and nose.

My daughter chokes and cries and becomes the shyest I've seen her when she's offered some water. She shakes her head no to the nurse and buries her face in my chest, falling asleep.

My cramped arm's about to do the same as the door cracks again.

"Gawd, Dust." Renata covers her mouth as she whispers as not to wake Sylvie. "Your text had me so worried. I couldn't get here fast enough." She looks at me as if she understands how hard it was for me to send Cece as her ride.

I'm glad she's gone home. I didn't feel like seeing her at the factory building, and I don't have the time to humor whatever sorry explanation I'll get if she stayed.

As soon as we have the test results, I'm bringing Renata and Sylvie home. The doctor comes back, putting a monkey wrench in my plan.

My body wants to bolt up and past him, marching out of the hospital. He holds up two hands and I adjust my immense frame in the minuscule chair.

"She's got strep, but Sylvie's also testing positive for the flu. Has she had her flu shot?"

"She always does. Her other grandmother has cancer and we want our visits with her to be as safe as possible. Not spreading germs and stuff." Renata speaks for me.

"Interesting. It's not unheard of to get the vaccine and still get influenza. The two combined are concerning. Not hugely, but Sylvie's also dehydrated. I'd like to keep her overnight for observation. Not being alarmist or intending to worry you, but it's a lot for her system to fight off, and I don't want to see it turn into pneumonia."

I appreciate the doctor's overabundance of caution, even though my pulse ratcheted, worrying over those percentages my child could get worse.

Sylvie's got a room and she hardly let out a peep when they put the IV in. My heart's breaking, feeling like the worst dad ever. How did this come on so fast, and how did I miss the signs?

Renata's sitting in a reclining hospital chair that doubles as a bed for caregivers. I hate being used to seeing her like this. She stayed in the same style chair for weeks after the car accident as I healed. I know she loves my daughter, but Renata literally got off the plane from her vacation and is back to taking care of us. It's unfair, she had retirement by the balls a few years ago.

I watch her eyes drift shut and spring wide open. "Oh, crap!" She sits up. Her shoes squeak on the tiles.

"What happened?"

"My bag!"

"Did you leave it in the car?"

"No, I left it with Celine. In the lobby."

"That was two hours ago!"

"Time flies when you're old, Dust. I lost track." She yawns, resigned to the long day.

"I'll go get it," I grunt, not wanting to do it at all.

"Make sure you thank her."

When I'm out in the hall on my way to the elevator bank, I take off the face mask printed with a clown smile on the front the nurse on this floor had given me.

Pitch black refracts everyone's movements in the windows of the lobby. Cece's dozing the way Renata was trying to do upstairs. She has her head propped in one hand. The other hand rests on the handle, protecting Renata's suitcase.

"You could have called." I startle her.

"I, uh, I haven't replaced—My cell is still in—There was no point to bringing it. It's dead."

She's worse than I am stammering through the explanation and I have no patience for it. Celine proved she was more concerned about the way our relationship looked to outsiders, how *I* look to them, to grant her any pity.

"Renata says thanks. You can go." I lift the handle of the bag, rolling it behind me.

Once again, the way I had been when I left Carver's

office earlier today, I'm sure it's the last time I'll have to deal with the mill or Celine Wescott and her apologies.

But you know what they say about best-laid plans.

Chapter Twenty-five

Celine

I'm sitting on Sylvie's bed, helping her peel off a shimmery mermaid from a page in a princess sticker book I got for her in the gift shop. I've only been here for a few minutes and Renata's been chatting me up about my day.

Sylvie looks loads better than she had at the mill. Her IV is out, and she's "pwomised"—oh, my goodness did that turn my insides gooey the way it had when she'd talked to her dad when we first met?—to drink all of her juice. She has even made an impressive dent in her supper.

I've also learned the doctor-on-call has decided Sylvie's staying one more night before she's discharged. It's loads more than I'd known since leaving here last night, which was a whole lot of nothing. Her dad hadn't even bothered to mention Sylvie was admitted. How's that for a "fuck you very much" when I'd volunteered to go to the airport and stuck around with Renata's stuff for a few hours.

There's an awareness with Dusty that I have what's

coming to me. But it's also hard not to feel hurt that I'd had to resort to having Gloria at the pediatric office do some sleuthing to find out how Sylvie was fairing today.

"She didn't turn the corner until after lunch," There's a courtesy in the way Renata speaks to me about her granddaughter. I'm not sure why I expect it now from Dusty other than he's always struck me as a better man than he's acted the past twenty-four hours.

"It kind of happens this way. Antibiotics take a day to kick in."

"Do this one next, please." Sylvie points to a redhead with a bow and arrow.

I lift it with my nail, cautious not to tear the edges. "This is harder than it seems." I smile, having fun. She asks which wilderness page she should affix it to and I blink at all the options since I've never done this before. My childhood thrill was if the bananas came with a blue sticker on them.

I've forgotten where I am and why we're here when Dusty growls walking into the cheery hospital room.

"What are you doing?"

The fine hair on my arms stand on end and I cross my legs. This isn't an appropriate reaction to a man who hates me.

"Celine was kind enough to bring our Sylvie a get well gift."

Scowling, he looks me up and down. "Want to talk. In the hall."

At first I'm certain he means me, but he pegs Renata in a stare and she gets up from her recliner.

"We'll be right back." She winks.

The wide door is open a crack and I'm doing my best to ignore the muffled voices. Sylvie's talkative. It gets quiet as she sticks her tongue out of her mouth and concentrates on sticker placement. That's when I hear Renata use a tone denoting Dusty should can his displeasure.

"I love you, Dust, but you're forgetting who that child's guardian is. You're letting your own mood get in the way of seeing Celine ain't here to bother no one."

He barges off, and she's back a moment later, rolling her eyes. "You stay as long as you want, sweetheart."

"Maybe a few minutes longer. It's getting late and I need to pack."

"Going someplace?"

"I'm moving." Against Sloan's advice. She's positive I need the support of friends at "a time like this" more than ever. I'm certain she's using it as an excuse to make me stay put.

"Far away?"

"Oh, no." I bat the air. "You know those townhouses they built a few years back about a mile from the highway ramp? A friend of a friend is leasing me theirs for the next year. They're relocating for work."

"I know right where you mean. Dusty's friend, Holly, lives there. It's not too big and they have a splash park for the kids during the summer."

"Holly's the one who helped me find it."

Renata's chin tips. "Sounds perfect since you've already met your neighbors. Best of luck."

"Thank you." I slide my purse onto my shoulder. "Well, if I don't see you anytime soon, get healthy, Sylvie Rhys." Her dad won't stand for a second visit.

A little yawn turns into a wide grin. She's got princesses stuck to her fingertips and wiggles each to say goodbye to me. I can't believe we're not going to have a chance to do this again.

One door may have closed, but I've left my bedroom door open, making it easier to pack. There's a pile of flat boxes stacked against the wall outside waiting for me to fold and fill them. A solitary one sits on my bed. I've placed a book inside because it was the closest thing within my reach, but glance around, taking in the sight of everything I've collected since moving in. It's not a lot, but each item is filled with memories and the idea of taking them out of their spots makes me tear up.

There's a rustle in the hall. Spine stiffening, my natural reaction is still that it's Dusty. A box slides down, laying at an angle on the carpeted floor. My breath is heavy as I fill my lungs. I'd prefer if my imagination stopped playing tricks on me. How long will it take to get over the anticipatory shivers waiting for his touch?

I pull a scarf down dangling over the mirror and ball it up before opening the top dresser drawer, filled with my costumes. My cheek bunches to the side. The irony that the G-strings are all so tiny they fit inside such a small space isn't lost on me. They've garnered me the cash to get to where I am. I'm not so prideful I'd never go back to dancing if times were tough, and I pull them out by the fistful and stuff them into the box.

My cell dings on the bedside table.

Carver: Know you're busy. Meet me on the stairs.

Won't take long.

Without responding, I place my phone down and walk out into the hallway, looking left. He's sitting beyond the red velvet rope on the last step before the landing wearing faded blue jeans and his signature crisp collared shirt. Casual meets GQ. His elbows are on his knees and his hands are clasped. He's patient, focused on the last rays of the late-day sun streaming through tall windows in the stairwell. It's strange Carver holds himself to his own rule.

"What can I do for you, Bossman?" I've called him this forever. Part of it's teasing because Sloan has funny nicknames for Carver. But, when it comes down to it and even though I worked for Jake, Carver's the one who runs the show.

"Have a seat," he chuckles.

"Okay." The whisper echoes off of the tall walls. "Am I in trouble?" I've been waiting for Carver to give me a piece of his mind.

"How's packing going?" He nods over his shoulder.

"Fine." *Does he want me out sooner?*

We watch a bird fly by the window.

"You've met Jake's mother, Caroline, right?" he asks.

"Yeah, she's a legend at the club."

Carver agrees. "I was a kid the first time I walked in there. Caroline became like a second mother to me. Lord has the answer to why. Jake was enough of a handful and she didn't need to take another brat on. She loved exotic dancing, which made her different from the rest of the ladies who worked there who had no other options and did it to scrape by. Caroline also was never jealous of the women who drew larger crowds. Ask me how I know."

"How do you know?"

"Because my mother was a headline act. While my mom was out doing all the things I hoped you wouldn't resort to, Caroline was feeding me dinner at her table. It left a big impression on me."

"I can see how it would."

"All the money my mother was supposedly making, all the random men who came in and out of our lives, she'd considered her meal ticket. But they also brought pain, heartbreak, and their own addictions along with them to share. It wasn't that my mother wasn't smart or capable of being like Caroline, it's that after one disappointment after another, she gave up." Carver pauses. "What did you want when Jake hired you?"

"First to pay my rent." I laugh, uncomfortably. "Then, watching Kimber graduate and fall in love with Trig, I wanted to prove to myself I could get there too." I shrug.

"Did you?" He's got a smirk and a hint of pride on his face.

"I got my degree and first professional job, wiiith the help of some good connections." Carver runs into Dr. Randolph on the golf course a lot.

"So you didn't get it all, though: Fall in love like Kimber had?" Carver doesn't wait for my response. "For what it's worth, Cece, I wish things had worked out between you and Dusty. You're both adults. I put a lot of faith in the people I let work around here, and I was sorry he chose to resign."

"But we broke your rules."

"I've bent plenty of them for Sloan." He shakes his head with a goofy grin as if he'd break every single one to make her happy.

I can't help the quirk of my lips.

"You don't have to leave. Not if you don't want to. There was never a steadfast deadline for anyone else. You're welcome as long as you want to stay."

"As much as I'll miss it here, I have to go. I've been holding onto the past. It's not helping me accomplish everything I'd hoped for when you offered me a place to stay."

"There's one thing you haven't crossed off your list." He makes the heart shape with his fingers.

"It's a moot point now. Dusty won't forgive me for showing my true colors. I don't blame him."

"Do you love him? Did we blow it for you both?" I hear the remorse in his voice.

"You, no. Morgan, probably. Me? Definitely. There was a sliver of truth in the way I reacted, and it proves I'm not ready to fall in love."

"I doubt anyone ever is. Maybe the lucky ones, but the rest of us get gobsmacked by it." Carver pats my knee, reassuring. "Tell me what you need help with."

"You've done too much already."

"Okay then. It's your turn."

My brow furrows, wondering if this is the moment I finally understand the intensity behind Carver's kindness. "What am I supposed to do for you?"

"Make sure Sloan knows I did everything in my power to talk you out of going. She's going to miss you, and no matter what you think, you're not replaceable. You'll always be welcome here if you need a place to come home to."

I keep the soft chuckle that Sloan put her man up to this to myself. "I will, and thanks for everything. Especially not—"

"Inserting my nose farther into your private business?" Carver runs a hand over his coiffed hair as he stands and pulls me up.

"That too." I give him a brief hug.

"Tell Skye when those boxes are full. He'll deliver them to your townhouse." Carver's halfway down the steps, back into boss-mode.

"Thank you," I repeat. The words of gratitude won't ever be enough.

I march my independent behind back down the hall. The first room I pass is Kimber's and it makes me pause. She's been gone for years and nobody has taken her place. I turn the knob to look inside. It's spotless with new bedding and linens in colors Kimber has decorated her house with. She'd love it.

I close the door, pondering over how all random things she leaves at the mill are down in the second-floor room Trig still keeps. The couple still sneaks down the hall when they are here. The space is overrun with their son's toys and, next to Jasper and Hailey's room, it's where Owen stays when they use Hailey as a sitter.

"Caroline left a big impression on me." Those weren't Carver's exact words, but they're close enough.

Jake's mom provided a parachute. Caroline caught him when times were the toughest. I finally understand a little of why I'm here and what Carver meant by saying we had a place to come home to.

Chapter Twenty-six

Dusty

Discharged from the hospital, my daughter is symptom free and ready to rejoin her kindergarten class at school. Me? All of a sudden, I'm the freak-show-first-day-of-school parent who can't cut the apron strings. Driving home misty-eyed, I belittle the choice to leave my baby out in the big wide world defenseless against the attack of ravenous wolves.

I love my girl with my whole heart, but watching women like Kimber, Aidy, Holly and she-who-won't-be-named find their callings, I'm also raising her to be independent. This need to protect and have Sylvie near isn't our norm. But like the doctor said, strep and influenza when a kid's gotten a flu shot isn't part of the everyday percentages.

I'm not even done triple-counting the number of days Sylvie missed and how many worksheets she'll have to catch up on tonight when our life hits another speed bump.

Pulling into the driveway, Renata's out on the front porch. At first, it seems as if she's wringing her hands—funny the nasty flashbacks that's giving me—but as I get out of the cab and approach the front stoop, I realize she's got her rosary in her hands. She's praying softly, slipping one bead at a time between the pads of her fingers.

Sitting down next to her, the old wicker chairs groan under my weight. When it comes down to it, I'm a scientist. I have faith but am not a religious man. However, I have hella respect for those who can give up control and place their lives in the hands of a creator. Renata is one of those   people. Her faith is a cornerstone of the woman she is and the choices she makes.

"Hospice called. Ben's mother passed." Her head stays bowed as she speaks to me.

"She was a wonderful woman." I place my palm on her knee and send a thankful vibe into the universe. Without Ben's mother there would have been no Ben, and without Ben I wouldn't be racking my brain over how to explain to my little girl her grandma has died.

"She was, Dust. She liked you. Don't matter what you believed then. Believe it now. After grieving your husband, you can come to understand why death takes one and not another, but the hardest thing ever is coming to grips with your child leaving this earth before you. Any negative feelings she had were never rejection. It was watching you be the man my grandbaby needed that she was so sure she'd get a chance to see Ben be. It's difficult to let go of what you thought your future was. All those plans up in smoke."

Losing Beth solidified Renata's friendship with Mrs. Yates. They'd been as tight-knit as sisters the past few years. So close, I'm positive Renata was the first person the nurse called with the bad news, even before Renata tells me she's got to see to the funeral arrangements.

Most of Mrs. Yates's last wishes are laid out as beautifully as she is for the wake. Other than fielding phone calls about where to show up and when, my mother-in-law doesn't have a lot to do past bringing the suit to the funeral parlor that Ben's mother will be buried in. I give her plenty of space throughout the day, though. We break the news to Sylvie together. She's got tons of hugs for Renata, and a few more days out of school.

After the burial, Renata and I sit side by side on hard white plastic chairs. We've stayed in the front row so the mourners have time to express their condolences, shake Sylvie's tiny hand, and tell her what an amazing person her paternal grandmother was.

I hope Sylvie remembers today. Other than a few distant cousins in attendance, she's the last of her line. Ben's family were decent folk. Saying otherwise is a blight on where my baby came from, and I won't disrespect her like that. Call it fate, or destiny, or God, I'm her father because something or someone out there had the foresight to intertwine my path with Beth's, allowing me to love a woman who was perfect for me.

Sylvie keeps taking off the coat I insist she needs to wear, telling us she's warm enough. I'm certain she's showing off the pretty dress Renata took her shopping for and I'm overreacting, worrying my daughter's going to catch something else. She's happy so I need to chill out and let her continue plucking flowers from each of the floral arrangements, making herself a bouquet from the largest blooms in each one. She'd done a great job of sitting during the service, and everyone wanting to speak to her so kindly made my girl feel like a princess on an extraordinarily sad day.

Renata dips her head to my shoulder. I turn, planting a kiss on the edge of her black pillbox hat. We're too caught up remembering what it felt like to lose Beth to do more than plaster on a weak smile. She pats my knee and we stare through the coffin as if it weren't there at nothing in particular.

"I want to talk to the lawyer tomorrow." Renata keeps her voice low so as not to wake the dead.

My eyes flick to the engravings on the headstone. Ben's dad's name is on the granite with his birth and death dates. His mother's birth year is there, but nothing else... yet. I look over the headstones, searching to where I know I'll find Beth. She's buried in this same cemetery next to her father.

I'm sort of surprised at Renata's comment since she was quick to put me down at the hospital and remind me that she was Sylvie's guardian. I hate admitting there's been a part of me that worried Renata wouldn't keep her promise. After all, I'm only the man who cut the cord, not the one who provided half of Sylvie's DNA. I have no claim to my child.

I wipe a tear with my knuckle and blame those misgivings on emotional overload. "Do you ever think it's a shame Beth's not with Ben?"

He was laid to rest in the state veteran's cemetery.

"No. I'm glad my Beth is with her daddy and that I'll join them. Some days I regret you won't lie alongside her when your days are done." Renata sighs. "Yet, I know someday up in heaven we'll all be together and it's what counts, not where our bodies rest."

"Ben and Beth were supposed to be it for one another."

"And they were, for a time. Then you stepped in and Beth found love again. Now it's your turn."

"Don't know what you're talking about, Renata. All I want is to go home so we can spoil Sylvie."

"Which is why I want to get those papers in order. I'm not sick or nothin', but I won't waste what time I have left. There's no sense dragging my feet, waiting to do what we all know is right. You are the only parent Sylvie's got. The only daddy she's ever known and Beth wouldn't forgive me if I let you slip out of Sylvie's life the way so many others have."

"It's too soon."

"If you could go back and do it all over knowing what

you know now, would you have married Beth sooner?" Renata asks.

I snuff back. Renata knows the answer. It hadn't seemed appropriate with Ben's death so fresh in everyone's mind. Beth's mother-in-law didn't not like me, she simply had a hard time with how fast I'd taken her son's place. Everyone was trying to heal in their own way. At their own pace. "We talked about it all the time."

"And before either of you knew, it was too late. So you've spent longer than you and Beth were even a couple, sleeping in my spare room, waiting for a chance to move on with your life and *your* daughter. At this point, all alone in my golden years, I'd only give my grandchild to a great man. You're a great man, Dusty. Worthy of the same second chance Beth got."

"We won't leave you." I choke out as Sylvie hands Renata the haphazard bouquet of roses, lilies, and wildflowers.

"Yes, you will. But you won't leave me *behind*." Renata's fingertips brush Sylvie's chestnut hair and she says a quiet thank you. Her faith has seen her through devastating losses over the past fifteen years. I'm sure her words of gratitude are as much for Sylvie's gift as the gift of Sylvie.

We stand and Renata loops her arm through mine, taking Sylvie by the hand. We make the slow march back to the car. The clouds part and the sun warms our backs. I'm never cold and hadn't realized the shade of the tent we'd sat under had created such a chill.

"Bring her back." Renata nudges my shoulder, not moving my solid form an inch.

"Who?" I act stupid.

"You know who." Renata pauses, facing me. "Dusty, stop worrying so much about what people think of you since the accident. Right now, the only thing hammering your cognitive abilities is testosterone.

You're being a stubborn man, pure and simple."

"I can't." The problem isn't bringing Cece back. It's if she'd come back to a guy who wouldn't hear her side of the story. I treated her like crap when she let bygones be bygones and put Sylvie first when she had the flu and I was oblivious. Well, not really oblivious, but my parenting guilt makes it feel that way. Not to mention, I yelled at her for showing up to check on a patient and bringing a gift. It startled me to see her at Sylvie's bedside. The way the two interacted was what I figured I'd be soon watching up in Boone since Cees and I had discussed the next steps in our relationship.

I overreacted when she made my ego question if I wasn't man enough for her. I lost my cool when she showed the compassion that attracted me to her in the first place. I'm also sure—after alluding to how her own mom and dad didn't quite excel at parenting, let alone the indications of what their marriage was like—I've fallen further down the ladder of acceptable men to date. Women like Cece Wescott pull themselves up by their bootstraps.

"Stop letting your pride overrule your heart. Beth didn't fall for you because you were an engineer and I doubt whatever attraction you and Celine have has a gosh darn thing to do with who you were before. She's friendly with the man you are now. While you did your best to keep whatever was going on between the two of you private, for some months you were happier than I've seen you since we lost Beth and she's the reason why. Celine is to you what you were to my daughter. Don't let a second chance slip away. I still have a family, but it's also a lonely life without someone to love."

I blow out a deep breath. "I wouldn't know the first way to fix the stuff between us, Renata."

"Don't go searching for a grand gesture to start anew. Sometimes the simplest answer is the one that does the best to start healing." She sniffs the flowers.

Chapter Twenty-seven

Celine

I had to run out during my lunch break to buy a new shirt and bra. Waiting for the cashier to ring me out, I'd believed as days go this one couldn't get worse. This morning I'd been spit up on by a newborn who had just nursed. Then, smelling like ode to curdled milk, I needed Gloria to help a mother restrain a toddler with a double ear infection so I could look in his ear with the otoscope without causing any more damage.

Snipping off the blouse's tag, I sliced the fabric near the back yoke and had to use a suture kit to repair the damage, which meant taking off the shirt and sitting in an exam room in my underwear. Gloria suggested making a matching hole in the opposite side and pretending it had blowout shoulders.

"Speaking of blowouts, with my luck today, the next baby I see will have a leaky diaper."

Gloria finds my joke hysterical, though I mean it.

"Your afternoon patients are all potty-trained."

This alone should help me relax, but my hackles raise entering an exam room and seeing the dad who was sure he recognized me. His daughter is back with a head cold. I check her ears and press under her tender cheeks to diagnose a sinus infection.

The only reason she's not squirming is because she feels awful. Meanwhile, the dad who also remarked she's been like this for days, hasn't been attentive at all to his child this time. He tries to chat me up. I respond to his questions about me with questions of my own about his daughter's health history. In an instant, his phone is more important than her cold.

Sure I've dodged a bullet, that's when he switches between whistling and humming "Sweet Caroline" by Neil Diamond.

The situation reeks worse than me smelling like baby puke in the line at the department store an hour ago. I close my eyes, able to breathe in my nose and out my mouth to maintain my professionalism since I have on a clean top.

I wash my hands and let him know the prescriptions she needs were sent to the pharmacy. Done with the exam, it's as if all three of us are trying to squish through the doorway into the empty hall at the same time. My hasty exit is like the rest of today, anything but easy.

"Go wait in the play area for me while I talk to the pretty nurse." The dad instructs his sick daughter.

At this moment, I can't correct his condescending tone or that he's gotten my medical degree wrong without kneeing him in the balls. So instead I place her file on the nurses' station countertop and pretend to go over my recommendations.

His child scampers away—to the germiest part of the waiting room—to spread more. I sigh and make a mental note to find the extra Lysol in the stockroom.

"I remember where I've seen you before." I can feel the heat of his gaze undressing me.

"How nice." I try to sound disinterested in catching

up.

His fingers rub the silky fabric over my forearm. "We could talk about this back in the exam room where it's a little more private. Play doctor?"

"Uh," *Gross* "no." My face twists. What did he expect? That I'd service him in a pediatric office?

"In that case, I'm not sure how I feel about someone like you treating my kids."

"Excuse me?" I step further away. "I can assure you, I am qualified."

He tries to invade my space again, but something comes over me the way it had when I wouldn't let Morgan degrade Dusty.

"It's also appropriate to tell you this facility makes patient safety a priority." I point up to the ceiling. "These video cameras are top of the line. Brand new actually. The firm my brother works for upgraded all the feeds this winter. He did most of the installation himself. Come to think of it," I touch my fingertip to my lip twice. "I'm almost certain he mentioned it's the same system they're using at an upscale *strip club* in Brighton."

I see the gears clicking and steam come out of the father's ears as they do. I want to make a snarky comment that using all that brainpower must be difficult for a dumbass like him. I mean, what man hits on a former exotic dancer and a split-second later acts like an entitled family man?

Yet, people never dig far enough to see past what's on the surface, do they? For me, it was easy to ignore the fact that Dr. Randolph was an acquaintance of Carver's when he was the pediatrician I shadowed. When he offered me a full-time position on his staff and the office was having their security system upgraded, I chalked it up to coincidence. Now? Well, if it is as innocuous as dumb luck, I'm glad luck's on my side.

"You don't say." He tries to brush off the panicked

animal feeling.

"I do. You wouldn't happen to know the name of the club? It's right on the tip of my tongue."

"I'm sure I don't."

"Hmm... And I'm sure next time you're offered a choice of providers, someone else will be seeing your children. I assure you, the concerns you have that I'm not equipped to treat them appropriately have been heard." I turn my back as Gloria rounds the corner.

"Your afternoon going any better, Cece?"

"So good. So good. So good." I repeat loud enough for the dad scurrying away with his tail between his legs to hear.

"What was all that?" Gloria asks when the lobby door slams shut.

"Creep sent his kid away and tried to come on to me." I start laughing at the absurdity.

"Isn't he married? What an asshole."

"Can you do me a favor?"

"Sure, Hon, anything."

"Jot a note in both his kid's files that I'm not interested in having them on my patient load. I know it's not professional, but it's for the best. I'll follow up with the office manager and Dr. Randolph to tell them why."

"They'll understand." She assures me, logging onto the computer.

The rest of the afternoon passes in a blur. I get into my car and the smug satisfaction that I've handled the rude family man has dissipated. If I were on my way back to the factory, Sloan and I would be all over the topic. But since I'm now living alone in the condo there's no one to share the small victory with.

I go home to a new and unusual sense of loneliness. No one is outside of my bedroom distracting me with a late night chat session or yanking me away from Netflix and out of my sweatpants for a drink at the club.

I consider dropping by Holly's with a six-pack before remembering she's managing at Sweet Caroline's tonight. Laurel is in charge of their kids during her sister's shift. I could text or call one of my friends to say, "Can you get over the nerve of this guy?", but it somehow lacks in comparison.

I'm low on food, and sitting alone in the big living room all evening isn't as appealing as the freedom having my own place seemed while I was finishing college. I stand by my word, it was time for me to leave the mill and venture out on my own. I'd accepted Carver's generosity too long and need to be an independent adult.

Adults eat at Wafflehaus as long as they do it before midnight, right?

I pick a location between the medical park and the condo, which doesn't take me too far out of my way. A waitress about my age takes my order. I put my cell by my silverware while I wait on my dinner. Instead of scrolling, my eyes travel the patterns in the Formica tabletop. I get lost in the highlights of the gold flakes against the blue-gray veins in the faux marble. Ten minutes have already passed, and the waitress is back. She sets a plate of French toast in front of me and offers to refill my drink.

I'm not the hugest coffee drinker and cover the mug with my hand so she doesn't pour any more in. The caffeine will keep me up and, for as victorious as I'd felt earlier, now I want to crawl into bed. Isolation has had me nit-picking my behavior and choices. The asshat father's opinion this afternoon bubbled every self-conscious thought I squelch during work hours to the surface.

I'm forced to admit, reevaluating my life requires more effort than eating the entire side of skillet home fries with onions and bell peppers on my plate. But at least I'm coming to grips with why my food can't touch.

One word: Casseroles. When it's all you're served as a kid seeing protein, starch, and vegetables as separate dishes is all-consuming. In theory, did I take it too far? *Duh.*

I'm dining alone in a greasy spoon because I wasn't ready for two things at once, and they would've been tasty had I given them a try.

A shadow passes by the door and I glance up from my next forkful of eggs and bread with drippy syrup. The air gets sucked out of the room.

Filling the threshold, Dusty searches for a booth. He notices me. His chin dips and my heart breaks. I see his shoulders slump as if he's about to step back and turn to leave. But Dusty sighs, resigned to be the better man, and acknowledges I'm here.

Spine straight, he walks between the booths, making the tiny diner feel smaller. I shrink a little in my seat and put the fork on my plate. My back stiffens as my flat palms press into the cracked red naugahyde seat cushion.

"Mind if I sit?"

I nod across the booth, wishing he'd said my name in the deep timber he uses. It's strange how much I'd felt like I was going to get to know about this man. I'd kept him at arm's length and the distance between us is so much further now than the physical expanse separating us. His knees don't even knock into mine the way they had under the table in the kitchen the morning Dusty had made me breakfast up in Boone.

"Haven't seen you here before."

"Haven't been to this location before or any of them this early."

"More of the late-night crowd?"

"I used to be."

"Breakfast is good any time of day."

With a shake in her hips, the waitress strolls up with a pot asking if Dusty wants coffee. It's obvious she's affected by him. I can't blame her. The man is handsome, and the way his shirt binds across his biceps had always made me certain Dusty could have any woman he wants.

His eyes meet mine, searching for an awkward approval signaling I'm fine with him staying. I nod and he tips his cup up, letting the waitress fill it. He tells her he needs a few minutes to decide on the menu.

When she hears him speak, she glances at me. Her discomfort is obvious. She expects me to translate what Dusty is saying. While punctuated, it's perfectly clear. There's nothing unfriendly in my stare back at the waitress, but it forces her attention back to Dusty in a "wanna make something of it?" way. She gives him a wary smile and tells him to flag her down after he's made a choice.

"Didn't mean to interrupt your meal." He encourages me to eat before it gets cold.

Despite the flip-flop my stomach does, I dig back into the plate. The next bite is mid-air when he rests his elbows on the table and asks, "What's your name?"

Chapter Twenty-eight

Dusty

"My name?"

Cece's dark lashes bat in confusion. I must be acting as if I'm not all there. I'm not, or rather, I haven't been for this woman. Renata was right. Where I've been is a mile ahead. The thing is, I've also been angry over the fallout and I haven't been sure I wanted to give Cece a chance to catch up.

When I walked into Wafflehaus and saw her across the restaurant, my first reaction was to turn around, go home, and make a ham sandwich. The same way Sylvie and I have daddy/daughter dates, she's out with her grandma tonight and I stopped here for a quick bite on my way home from the hardware store.

There's a bag in my daughter's booster seat with parts I need for my next project. I've been hiding out at Renata's, getting around to a few things I've wanted to fix. Laurel texted to see if I'd re-key her front entry. I agreed as long as it was during a weekday. One of Renata's friends asked if I'd replace some boards on their back porch. Both gigs are a decent way to stay busy since I like what I've been doing the past few years. I haven't found a full-time job yet and, at some point, I'll have to hash it out with Carver. If your paycheck comes direct deposit, it's hard to refuse to cash it.

We both know I don't need the money and it's Carver's way of leaving the door open in case I change my mind and want to come back. The day I quit, I meant what I'd said to Morgan. He'd been so amped up, so angry, it wouldn't have taken much for him bursting in to turn tragic. But I'd also refused to see my role in any of this beyond being the good guy who got the raw deal.

Had I once in the past year said to my buddy, "I'd like to ask your sister out?" No, what I'd done was make sure that reality and the one I pretended to be content living in hadn't intersected. Bucking up the courage to run it by my friend, and having him laugh in my face, was along the same lines as Cece rejecting me.

Morgan had trusted me in the beginning and his perception changed the more Cece and I hid what we were doing. Even if Morgan guffawed, I know now Cees had been waiting on me to get off my ass and do it. She would've said yes. Her brother might have perceived my actions as less stalkerish. The way he is about keeping Cece safe, he may have even reacted the opposite way. While I'm certain things not working out between Celine and me has become a huge thorn in everyone's side, letting your sister date someone who can defend her in a back alley is a safe bet.

A little lightbulb goes off over Cece's head when she figures out nothing I've said to her so far denotes we know one another. "Celine." She gives me a reticent smile

"Pretty. Anyone give you a nickname?"

"My friends call me Cece, but this guy once called me Cees. It always made my world stop."

She'd never shared that. I have to take a sip of caffeine to restart my heart. "Hmm... You seem like the unstoppable sort... determined... like you have a damned serious direction you're headed in."

Cece scratches her neck behind her ear, looking away with endearing shyness. The club's clientele notwithstanding, Cece hasn't had a ton of experience with guys. If I'd paid more attention I would have known demure Cece is the real her. She's in a passenger car with an itinerary and stops before she makes it to her destination. I'm riding more of a freight train, full speed ahead.

I'd accepted Beth disembarked and grieved that loss. She and I had been traveling the same route. Beth hadn't forced fatherhood on me. I was all in the day I became a dad. And as the pain of losing Beth subsided, I hadn't liked my love life sitting at the station. Then Cece came along and my feelings for her grew. It was an express ticket.

I pushed for dinner at Royce's when she conveyed interest in midnight pancakes at Wafflehaus with a side of bacon. Before either of us had a chance to digest our first date, I forced her into a romantic weekend away. I've known all along Celine Wescott belongs by my side, but I've been trying to speed her up and drag her to where I am. I haven't even been willing to go back a few paces and meet her halfway.

So seeing her at the place she would have come to with me months ago, it's clear to me; This is the last second chance we're getting.

"Dusty." I give her my name and tap my temple. "I, uh, had an accident a few years back. It affects my speech. It's all up here, though." I know she knows this, but we can't go back the way we were. This is a fresh start. "Tell me about you."

"Okay..." She rubs her palms on her slacks. "I ah, work in a pediatric office and." She pauses, gnawing on her lip. "Dusty, I need to be upfront. I just got out of a relationship and it ended horribly. I did a lot of things wrong. So. Many. Things. The biggest is not being honest about my feelings. My mother is an addict and I chose to use her drug habit as an excuse to hide how terrifying it was I'd never felt worthy of his attention. Also, I'm trying to get over being a tad bit compulsive."

I huff with a wolfish grin. I like the direction the conversation is going in and see Celine's apology for what it is. "This guy?" I prod.

"He was different than most men, and I wasn't sure how I could stand up for him. I was ashamed to have those thoughts. Then everything changed. It was a literal slap in the face when I realized he was a man I was ready to fall in love with, and it was too late."

She gathers her hands to her chest to wring them, but I catch one before they're clasped. She stares at how easily our fingers lace together.

"While we're being honest." I clear my throat and Cees lifts her gaze to me. "I was sure the last woman I was with was a piece of work when I broke it off. I was mad for her... Completely insane since I already knew I loved her. But I was loving the person I wanted her to be and not the person she kept trying to remind me she was. I pushed her too quick. My accident changed my perspective. I don't take things for granted. Time is finite. But everyone has their own timeline, right? You can't rush people into things they're not ready for. Had I taken a better opportunity to get to know her, she'd have helped me understand I needed to be as patient with her as she is with me."

Cece brushes a fat tear trailing down her cheeks. I cup one side of her face, wanting to kiss it away. We both know it's too soon. We settle for the way she nuzzles toward my palm and the way it whispers how much we've missed one another.

"So pediatrics... Are you a nurse?" I go back to

pretending this woman is new to me because so many parts of her are.

"Physician's assistant."

"Like kids? I have a daughter. We're looking for things to do now that the snow's gone in the mountains."

"Has she ever been to Pullen Park? There's a lot to do there. The Carousel is beautiful."

"Yeah, Sylvie likes the dobby horses and the paddle boats."

"My brother is all about the train." She tests the waters with a grimace.

"He ride it a lot?"

"Not as a kid. All the time with his girlfriend's brother." Cece laughs, giving me something to rib Morgan about. But I'd just assume ask Morgan if he wants to tag along with Owen and ride next to me and Sylvie.

"Interested in going sometime?"

"I'm free this weekend?" she replies hesitantly.

"Cees," I pull her lip away from her tooth. "Can't do this slow if you're going to maul your face and make me want to kiss you."

Her mouth makes a pretty little 'o'. "How slow?"

"Only as fast as it takes to fall in love."

"For someone who says they have trouble speaking you know the right thing to say."

"Are you ready?" The waitress is back, intent Cece's the one placing my order.

I haven't taken my eyes off of my girl's smile and she won't look up at the waitress, forcing the other woman's attention to my side of the booth.

"Dust," Cees squeezes my hand and says loud enough for me to hear, "I'm ready if you are?"

"I'll have what she's having."

The streetlights have been on for hours and the late crowd is descending on the Wafflehaus when I walk Cece outside the restaurant. We stand in the now vacant parking spot separating our vehicles. There was a van blocking my view of her car before. I'd like to fill the owner's tank. If I'd seen it there, I would have driven by and spent the night alone brooding instead of enjoying it with this woman.

"I had fun. Thank you, Dusty."

"Glad they had ice cream once all that dinner digested. And chocolate sauce on yours? Impressive headway."

"I aim to turn your worst impressions of me around." She lets out a self-deprecating laugh, making me grin.

It's been amazing to be with her again the way we had been up in Boone. We've gone back-and-forth pretending to know and not know one another all night. Honestly, I can't wait for a repeat, but I need to take it slow for Cece's sake if this relationship is going anywhere.

"Listen, I um…" Rubbing my neck, I see Cece's line of vision dart to my biceps and opt to stretch out the kinks from sitting so long. She's always had a thing for the muscles in my arms and, if she's teasing me with those lip bites, then I'm doing the same. "I meant what I said about a picnic in the park this weekend. It can just be us—"

"Sylvie is welcome. I'm glad to hear she's feeling better, and I'd like to spend some time with her."

"You would? There's no rush."

"I don't feel pushed, Dusty." She places a palm over my heart and I draw her into my arms, nestling my nose to the spot behind her ear. She sighs and I'm back to being certain Cece is where she belongs.

When I pull away, she's got a come hither look. "Follow me home?"

"What do you take me for," I taunt, "some jerk who buys a girl a fancy dinner and fucks her in a parking lot in the front seat of his truck?" Her chest shakes as I press my lips to her forehead, whispering how sorry I was for being that guy.

"I miss you so much when you're not around," she confesses.

"Miss you too, Cees. But if this is a do-over, we're doing it right. Sex is a second date sort of thing, and we've only met." I wink.

"Are you implying I'm being impatient?"

"Nope, reminding myself great orgasms come to those who wait."

"That was awful!" She covers her nose as she snorts.

"It was... But us, Cees? We're perfect for one another. Wait and see."

Dusty

"I wanna go tooo." Sylvie drops dramatically to the ground. Her play medical bag stethoscope unwinds from her neck.

"Crocodile tears," Renata mutters. "You're going to give me a complex."

My chest rumbles as I pick my daughter's limp body up off the living room carpet. Her limbs hang like a rag doll's, but she's quick to snag the pink and blue stethoscope from the floor.

"What's that?" She clings to me to get her way. I can't say I blame her.

"It means you're breaking my heart, making me feel like you love Miss Celine more than me. And I'm your grandma!" Renata throws her arms in the air, using as much flair to toss a dish towel over her shoulder.

"I love you both!" Sylvie's lip wobbles. She doesn't realize Renata's pulling her leg.

"Of course you do." Renata makes gimme hands and Sylvie launches herself from my arms to her grandma's like a monkey jumping from a tree. Renata winks at me.

She's got this down pat and I can't help grinning back.

"I still wanna see Cece." She puts the earpieces in. *Hero worship much, kid?*

"Tomorrow, Peanut." I lift the bell and talk into it. "Cece misses you too."

She places the bell over my heart and I notice she's wearing the plastic bandage like a bracelet.

"Am I sick?"

"Yes."

"Okay then, I shouldn't be late. Cece will know what to do."

"Daadddeee."

I worried a lot about how Cees and me trying again would affect my daughter. We went out on a few dates to ensure the spark wasn't our imagination. About six weeks ago we took Sylvie to Pullen Park on a gorgeous spring day. I'm getting to the point that life without the two of them seems so far in the rearview we'd have trouble finding the road back. Not a huge problem for me.

"I can't even wait that long." Sylvie slumps.

"You can. Now stop. Miss Celine doesn't act like this when it's your daddy/daughter date night."

Sylvie's spine straightens. She cups Renata's cheeks and looks her dead in the eyes as if what her grandmother has said is an epiphany. Scrambling down, Sylvie yells for me not to leave until she's back with the card she drew for Cece this afternoon. It is decorated in princess stickers, and animal stickers, and shimmy star stickers, even the stickers that come off the bananas from the grocery store. Don't ask me what the sticker bond is between the two of them. It's their thing. Tomorrow is sticker day. Renata's got plans and I have to work for a few hours to finish up a project for a client. Cees offered to watch Sylvie. It's not the first time I've left them together, and the way Sylvie reacted when she found out, I have no doubt it won't be the

Epilogue

"I wanna go tooo." Sylvie drops dramatically to the ground. Her play medical bag stethoscope unwinds from her neck.

"Crocodile tears," Renata mutters. "You're going to give me a complex."

My chest rumbles as I pick my daughter's limp body up off the living room carpet. Her limbs hang like a rag doll's, but she's quick to snag the pink and blue stethoscope from the floor.

"What's that?" She clings to me to get her way. I can't say I blame her.

"It means you're breaking my heart, making me feel like you love Miss Celine more than me. And I'm your grandma!" Renata throws her arms in the air, using as much flair to toss a dish towel over her shoulder.

"I love you both!" Sylvie's lip wobbles. She doesn't realize Renata's pulling her leg.

"Of course you do." Renata makes gimme hands and Sylvie launches herself from my arms to her grandma's like a monkey jumping from a tree. Renata winks at me.

She's got this down pat and I can't help grinning back.

"I still wanna see Cece." She puts the earpieces in. *Hero worship much, kid?*

"Tomorrow, Peanut." I lift the bell and talk into it. "Cece misses you too."

She places the bell over my heart and I notice she's wearing the plastic bandage like a bracelet.

"Am I sick?"

"Yes."

"Okay then, I shouldn't be late. Cece will know what to do."

"Daadddeee."

I worried a lot about how Cees and me trying again would affect my daughter. We went out on a few dates to ensure the spark wasn't our imagination. About six weeks ago we took Sylvie to Pullen Park on a gorgeous spring day. I'm getting to the point that life without the two of them seems so far in the rearview we'd have trouble finding the road back. Not a huge problem for me.

"I can't even wait that long." Sylvie slumps.

"You can. Now stop. Miss Celine doesn't act like this when it's your daddy/daughter date night."

Sylvie's spine straightens. She cups Renata's cheeks and looks her dead in the eyes as if what her grandmother has said is an epiphany. Scrambling down, Sylvie yells for me not to leave until she's back with the card she drew for Cece this afternoon. It is decorated in princess stickers, and animal stickers, and shimmy star stickers, even the stickers that come off the bananas from the grocery store. Don't ask me what the sticker bond is between the two of them. It's their thing. Tomorrow is sticker day. Renata's got plans and I have to work for a few hours to finish up a project for a client. Cees offered to watch Sylvie. It's not the first time I've left them together, and the way Sylvie reacted when she found out, I have no doubt it won't be the last.

Sylvie's literally got her palms on my backside, pushing me out the front door. I have the impression she thinks the sooner date night is over, the quicker she gets her alone time with Cees.

Renata asks me to stop to get the mail before I take off. I nod. We've been waiting on some official paperwork. I pull the wide envelope with the state seal on it out of the box. Tapping it on the leaflets and magazines, my heart swells. I hold it up for Renata to see and confirm it arrived. She blows me a motherly kiss and waves goodbye, dropping the curtain.

Given our circumstances, Renata and I have gone out of our way to make Sylvie's life as normal as possible. It wasn't until Cece opened up about her childhood that I began to give any thought to how little control Sylvie felt she had over the way we lived. I hesitated changing her last name. For me, Ben and Beth are a huge part of her. I'm grateful every day for my daughter, but even Renata reminds me the memories she has of them are the stories we keep alive, not experiences Sylvie remembers. She wants to be an Alston because in her mind it unites us. Renata and I struck a deal to tell Sylvie her last name is Alston on her birthday, which is coming up soon. Now that I understand my little girl's perspective, it's hard to squelch the secret that I really am her daddy and no one can separate us.

There's only one woman I want to show the envelope to more than my daughter, but my cell rings, interrupting the thought. Instead of letting it go to voicemail, I take the call. Last month, I hung a shingle as a skilled handyman. Business took off like a shot. It's why I have to work in the morning.

This person's looking for an estimate, and I set up an appointment for next week. Before ending the call, I ask where they got my contact information. The fact that almost everyone's referral is from the same source means I need to put a stop to it. I shoot off a text to Cece saying I'm running late, but am on my way.

I swing by the mill on my way through Brighton. It's early evening and the factory's front entrance is still open. I loop through the lobby, and down the hall, rapping on Carver's door. It's ajar, so I have a feeling he's expecting someone.

"Come in."

"This has gotta stop."

Carver looks at me blankly.

"The direct deposit. The referrals. I don't want them." It seems in addition to keeping me on payroll, Carver had been dropping my name around Brighton to help build my list of clients.

He leans back in his plush leather chair. "The banking matter is something you'll need to discuss with Skye. The money is profit from your investment. Since you'd refused to speak to me, Skye decided to pay it out piecemeal. His intent was to make it look like earned income to the taxman until you'd calmed enough and were ready to talk turkey. It's damn hard to hide that kind of money otherwise, but obviously Skye manages."

"What the hell is he investing in?" I scrub my face. "No, don't tell me." I'd tried to keep my nose clean around here.

"I won't then. You can ask Skye the questions you want. I only okayed it after he reassured me that the tax rate was lower parsing it out to you in small increments. The rest of your gains are—"

"Offshore."

"You said that, I didn't. All I will mention is reinvested or not, it will take effort to spend down the profits given the current rate of return."

"I didn't ask you for this."

Carver's jaw squares. "If you want clean hands, Skye will figure out the logistics. As for the recommendations, I was hoping to right a few wrongs.

I'm sorry if I overstepped my boundaries and made you uncomfortable or to think there were any strings attached. The way everything went down was unfair. I have a great deal of respect for you, Dusty. You're one of us and we wanted you to be successful."

I sit in a chair across from the man I've known since we were kids. Carver was never one of the people asking why I wanted to be an engineer. He was the one who listened to how I planned to become one.

Leaning in on my elbows, I lay it on the line. "I'm busy tomorrow finishing a build for a new customer."

"Great."

"No, man. All I want is enough work to stay busy while Sylvie is at school. Cece is at work. Now they're doing some crazy sticker book madness. Meanwhile, I'm busting my ass while they're having fun. Not taking on employees. Already can't keep up with new jobs. You're killing both our reputations. For what?" I point towards Skye's cave where he makes all the number magic happen. "You told me my finances are solid. Damn it, if I gotta spend the next twenty years looking over my shoulder… Wor-rying Uncle Sam's possibly coming after me for tax evasion… At least give me a chance to enjoy the money I earned. Can't even get up to Boone to work on my own house at this rate."

"I hadn't realized you were gunning to spend more time at home. You sort of left without telling us what you were going to do. If you're only looking to keep busy, I have an opening for a handyman."

"Not coming back, Carver." I'm upfront. "I appreciate what you've done for me, but it's time to move on."

"Funny, Cece said something similar." We stand and clasp hands. "Talk to Skye. And don't be a stranger." Carver looks down at his desktop, then back at me. "You were a friend long before this, Dusty."

"We still are." I doubt I won't spend the next decade in his company. I just don't want to work for it. I also won't ask the woman I love to give up her network of friends. She's close to the women who are connected to every one of the men here.

On my way out, Morgan is hustling down the staircase, twirling his keyring around a finger. My discussion with Carver hadn't lasted long, but I'm surprised to see Cece's brother still here.

He comes to a standstill when his shoes hit the lobby floor.

"Cece called to say you were running late. I'm on my way to get Aidy."

I acknowledge his words with a grunt and chin lift. We're testing the waters, trying the double-date thing tonight. Cece and Aidy planned the evening. They want to eat at the Mongolian restaurant. Morgan and I are along for the ride.

"So, uh." Morgan rubs his scalp and motions to the door uncomfortably.

"Should have told you how I felt about Cece." It's better for Morgan and I to have it out now than the possibility either of us cause a scene later.

"I did a bad job of keeping my own insecurities out of it." Morgan acknowledges my apology. "Dust, bad shit went down before Celine hooked me up with Carver. The kind of bad shit that's all over the news about the Pinewood College rape cases..." Morgan looks defeated. "Aidy and me, we're talking to a counselor. But sometimes it gets the best of me that I can't stop those things from happening. Cece was all alone while I was in jail. She had no one."

"She had her mill girls." I disagree, but add, "That's why you walked her home," when the reality of Morgan's over protectiveness hits me.

Another reason Morgan brandishing the gun bugged me so damned much was, for all the illegal crap the factory walls hide, it's not Carver's way. You'd be a fool to walk into this building and not notice how much money is here, or maybe how much money *isn't* in a posh place like this. Mill business hides white collar crime. These men may have a side piece, but they're not running illegal firearms or drugs and I'm ninety percent certain that's a conscientious choice since mill girls hooking is frowned upon. I mean, combine Sweet Caroline's with the factory's dormitory-style bedrooms and this place could be the Best Little Whorehouse in Brighton. And it's not.

"I projected the fear that my sister wasn't safe on you. It took over. So every incident ramped my suspicion."

I hold up a hand to stop Morgan. He doesn't need to explain any further. I can picture myself overreacting when it comes to the women in my life. Hell, I'd held my breath driving under overpasses after losing Beth. Experiences like those change you. "We're good. Except one thing."

"What's that?"

I lay out our truth for Celine's brother. "Someday— when she's ready—I'm marrying her."

"Do I get an invite to the wedding?"

"Man, you're walking her down the aisle," I say because it's obvious that's what Cees would want.

"Nobody I'd trust more to give my sister to and keep her safe." Morgan claps me on the back.

Celine

"Faster!" Sylvie shrieks. "They're beating us!"

We're neck and neck with Holly. She and her son skid down the next lane over from ours. I've lost count of how many times we've raced. Still, we're both hooting and whooping with glee.

It's late in the season on a gorgeous sunny day in the mountains. This afternoon has been the kind where you almost feel ridiculous for wearing snow pants. My jacket is unzipped and the wind whips past my face, cooling me off as we whizz down the hill.

Sylvie, decked out in pink and purple snow gear, is in the front of the two-person tube. The honey-colored braids I put in her hair this morning flap back toward me, slapping at her shoulders as the heavy skid plates slow our speed when Bowe reach Cthe end of the ride.

Both she and Bhodi jump from their spots and clamor toward the poor teenager who keeps watch on the tuber's safety at the bottom of the run.

"Who came in first?"

He shrugs as if he's used to this kind of kid's

competition and smartly tells them it was a tie.

"Once more?" They beg, exhilarated and exhausted. Sweat drips down their foreheads.

"This was the once more!" Holly reminds them with as much exuberance. "Everyone else already left. They're waiting on us. Dinner isn't cooking itself."

I bite my tongue before blowing it and saying the opposite is true. The smokers and crockpots have been on all day. It's why making the kids happy by staying behind for a bit longer was an easy choice to make.

Holly and I stow the tubes. On the trek toward the parking lot, our kids whine for the first fifty feet before they're colluding. They conclude leaving doesn't mean the party is over. They're switching to their swimsuits to use the hot tub once we are back at the house.

"Mom, I'm hungry," my daughter declares on the ride home in Dusty's truck.

From the passenger seat next to me, Holly swipes two bananas from a knapsack. She hands them back to the kids like six-shooters making *pew-pew* noises.

"Thanks," Sylvie says. "Oh, I got one!" She leans forward, affixing a sticker upside down to my parka.

"I love it, Chiquita!" I tell her. She's getting old for sticker books, but blue produce stickers will always be our thing. When Sylvie has her own child—someday far, far, down the road—I hope, even if they don't maintain the tradition, this is a memory she shares. I also have every last one of her teeth that have fallen out so far. They're tucked away with my own.

The road curves and I press the brake, slowing to turn onto our property. There are still a few weeks before the leaves bud, but we still have a good deal of privacy before the driveway opens up to the field where the house stands.

Last year was lucrative for everyone at the mill. Dusty and I used the investment portfolio profits to add on to the little cabin in the mountains. We wanted to spend more weekends up here and had outgrown the space we had.

"Hon, this place is so impressive. I'm so happy for you, but it might kill me if you move out here all the time." Holly spends her vacations at the beach.

"It's a someday plan." I smile, pulling up behind a myriad of other vehicles parked in our driveway.

"You and your plans," she pokes fun at me on our way inside. "Throw a little caution to the wind."

"If we did that, we would be here permanently."

Holly trails her lacquered fingertips over the hood of a classic station wagon with shiny chrome accents. It's all her. A full ski rack is on the top. "Then forget I mentioned anything," she calls over her shoulder as we're greeted by a houseful of guests.

I can't believe how lucky we are to have such good people in our life to share our mountain home with. This is the first chance Dusty and I have had to entertain our friends in Boone. The contractor met with the building inspector and took down the building permits on Monday. The furniture for the guest rooms got delivered in the nick of time.

We had the ceiling in the living room vaulted and a two-story addition put on the opposite side of the house. Dusty's done the lion's share of the finish work because he had a vision of how he wanted it to turn out —a plan I teased him mercilessly about when he took an extra month to approve the architectural designs, unable to decide on how many garages we needed.

The answer is three. One for my car, one for his truck, and one for his tools.

Across the room, I can see smoke from the grills fired up on the back porch as my husband walks in through the open back slider. Kids of all ages mill about.

It smells of charcoal and barbecue and Dusty tastes like the scotch he, Trig, Cary, Carver, and Morgan are passing around.

"Have fun?" Dusty asks, tugging at my waist.

"Yeah." I glance around the living room to make sure everyone has what they need. Most of the girls are sitting on the couches, nursing glasses of wine.

"But?"

"I missed you." I worry my lip with subtle intent.

"How can you miss daddy? He's right here!" Sylvie flails her arms in the air like a duck.

"If you're using the hot tub, get your suit on now," I instruct her. It'll get cold once the sun goes down and not everyone is staying at our place. A few booked rentals by the nearest ski resort. "Bhodi's leaving at bedtime."

I turn my attention back to her father.

"Missed you too." Dusty grins, dipping his lips to my ear. He whispers naughty words and that his intent would be to strip me out of the ski pants I've got on if guests weren't here.

Bhodi and our daughter zip between us with towels.

"Sorry, Uncle Morgan!" I hear before a big splash on the deck as they dive into the water.

Seeing my brother coming, Dusty pecks me on the lips and goes in search of his favorite grilling tongs.

"Do they always have this much energy?" Morgan asks, holding a jumping baby out to me.

"Yes, they do. They do. They do." I baby talk to the chunky eight-pound, twelve-ounce baby girl I delivered last year. The spitting image of her daddy, Delilah is even bigger now. Dusty's daughters are my entire world, and he's the universe. The one thing I have more faith in than anything else is my marriage because of my husband's faith in me.

"Ma-Ma-Ma-Ma," Delilah squeals as I brush our noses together.

Then I give my brother a smarmy look that he returns with a smirk.

"Oooh, your time is coming!" I taunt. "Make sure

your wife has a water bottle while I change your niece's diaper."

Dusty's strong calloused palm tugs on my thigh, spreading my legs, and he works his magic on my clit. Somewhere between sleep and awake, I let out a needy whimper. Bucking into the sensation from the three fingers he uses to ready me, it doesn't take much before I'm soaked. He bites my shoulder; a gentle reminder to keep my voice down. I look through the crack of our door to where the one for the girls' room is shut.

Once they've grown a little older, the plan is to move the girls into their new rooms for more privacy. But for now, I like having them close—Bathroom rendezvous are commonplace. So thank goodness we have experience, and a lock.

His hand moves, cupping my pussy.

"No, don't stop," I beg for more of the stretch I love, rubbing his rigid cock through his sleep shorts.

"Mmm... Cees. Wanted to fuck you all day." His warm breath blows past my ear. His fingers go back to massaging my cunt.

I sneak my hand below the elastic waist of Dusty's pants, trying to pleasure him as much as he is me. "I want all of you," I whisper, greedily.

Dusty sheds his only article of clothing. He maneuvers between my legs, pushing my knees open and shoving up my top. After palming my breasts, he thrusts inside of me, covering his body with mine.

"Shh... You'll wake the house," he chastises, covering my mouth with his lips. With slow steady thrusts,

Dusty brings me to the brink, making up for the hours apart this afternoon while we entertained.

Like molasses in the winter, it takes me a while afterward to move. I pad to the bathroom to clean up. While I'm in there, the baby starts crying.

I search for my ratty gray sweatpants in the dark. By the time they're over my hips, Delilah has settled. Still, I tip-toe out of the master bedroom, telling Dusty I'll be back soon.

It's surprising to find the door to the girls' room open and Delilah's crib empty. I hear a sound in the kitchen and follow the soft ray cast by the light.

"I hope you don't mind. She seemed to want to be held." Aidy leans against the sink with Delilah straddling her baby bump.

A sippy cup in her mouth, my younger daughter twirls Aidy's shoulder-length red hair in the other for comfort. I often mix Aidy up with Kimber nowadays. It's still unusual to see Aidy without the streaks of lavender.

I tip-toe over and run my fingers through Delilah's dark sweaty locks. She's a hot sleeper. I was an inferno from the point I'd conceived. No test needed, I knew Dusty had left a piece of himself to grow inside me. Realizing I was having a baby was one of the best moments of my life, next to telling Dusty, and us letting Sylvie know she was going to be a big sister.

"No, I was about to pick her up to snuggle anyway. Let me know if your arms get tired."

Aidy pats her swollen belly under Delilah's bottom. "We're using the bump for all it's worth."

"It's worth a lot." I hug Aidy from the side. I can't wait to meet my brother's child. I never met my own aunts and uncles and, in a million years, I hadn't expected we'd be raising babies alongside one another. "I'm so excited for you and Morgan."

I'm also envious. Dusty and I have talked about more,

but we're compromising, waiting until Delilah is out of diapers. Dusty's schedule allows him to be home with the girls as much as possible. I have guilt over pushing my luck. How many mothers are fortunate enough to have a sexy house husband and an amazing grandma like Renata who helps out at the drop of a hat?

"Thanks. I can't wait for this part." She looks dreamily at her niece. "Aaand the heartburn to be over."

"Is that what got you up?" I grimace. We had spicy southern barbecue with vinegar at dinner.

"No, sweetheart, what woke her was the same thing that woke everyone else who wasn't sleeping; You." Sloan sashays toward us with a wicked grin.

I cover my face, glad the dim lamplight hides the crimson seeping into my cheeks. "Sorry."

"You don't have to apologize to me. Carver wasn't ready to sleep either. There's something to be said for loving a man who takes care of your every toe-curling need." She winks in my direction, adjusting her robe as she sits down on a stool.

Aidy's snort startles Delilah. "Ma—" she bleats like a baby goat.

I reach for her, but Sloan says, "My turn," with gimme hands.

"When is your turn?" Aidy asks, watching Sloan cradle Delilah in her arms. "Morgan joked if Kimber and Trig have another they'll be saying there's something in the mill's water."

"Babies are catchy. We could start a mill-sponsored softball team," I suggest.

Our friend's age's run the gamut, but we're all as close as can be. It's not surprising we're all having kids at the same time.

Sloan rubs Delilah's feet through her sleeper. "My time passed."

"I find that hard to believe," I harrumph. "You'd be the best mother. It's not like you have zero experience with kids."

"If you mean Hailey, that's different. I should have managed the situation a lot better, and made more than my fair share of mistakes."

I'm trying my hardest not to but, "Isn't that part of the charm of parenthood? Saying we won't be like our own moms and dads and screwing our kids up in a completely different way?"

"Ugh, you should see the teens I deal with at the high school." Aidy shudders. "Maternity leave can't come soon enough."

"Are you going back after the baby is born?"

"Of course, I am. These kids need me!" Her voice raises enough to hear beyond the walls of the large room.

As our laughter fades, Carver appears shirtless on the landing to the second floor. His flannel pants hang low on his hips, showing off a delicious V. I'm all set to go back and enjoy the warmth of my bed and Dusty's company. Carver's physique gives Dusty's a run for the money, but he doesn't have those enormous pecs or massive biceps that keep me—

"I'm not drooling. And if I am, it's pregnancy hormones and neither of you are to tell Morgan," Aidy remarks beneath her breath. "Hi, Carver, what can we do for you?"

"I'd like my wife to come back to bed. We're here for two more days. If it's all the same to you, I'd rather not share her at midnight when you'll all be clucking tomorrow."

"Clucking?" I put my hand to my chest in mock horror. "I don't cluck!"

"No, you moan," Aidy titters. "Loudly."

"Really loudly," Sloan agrees.

I gasp at their cheek and hit Aidy's shoulder before taking my daughter back into my arms. Smiles hide our giggles.

Delilah sighs in her sleep again and my heart swells. It would be so great if Sloan could experience this.

"Sloan. Bed. Now," Carver orders.

"I'm coming, Mister Bossy Pants." Sloan's already slipped up the stairs, but he swats her ass for the flippant remark.

"I'm headed back to our room too." Aidy yawns and kisses Delilah's temple. "Sleep tight." She waves, disappearing into the darkness.

Swaying back-and-forth, I rock Delilah for a few minutes longer and bring her back to her crib. I pull the covers up over Sylvie, touch her damp and frizzy honey-colored braids, wondering how she'll want to wear her wavy hair in the morning. Then I kiss her the way Aidy had Delilah. "I love you, Sylvie Rhys."

"Love you, Mommy," she answers in her sleep.

Mommy. I'm their mommy.

This is not how I saw my future pan out. I thought I'd meet the man I'd make a life with after practicing medicine for a few years. I knew I wanted to be a mom, but never once considered my child would have another mother first. I was positive I'd mourn the loss of not ticking off everything on my checklist. Yet, what I wound up with was so much more.

I lean against the door jamb, soaking in the sounds of the quiet house settling in the cold. Dusty comes up behind me. His lips trail the nape of my neck. Our fingers intertwine as he pulls me back to our massive bed. I snuggle up next to him, absorbing the heat of his body. His palm caresses my lower belly, content to stay there. He'd held me like this while Delilah grew inside of me.

I take a deep breath.

"What're you thinking, Cees?"

"Baby?"

"The girls are fine."

"No, Dust. I want another one."

He moves his massive frame and the bed rocks. I can make out the silhouette of his bicep, shoulder, and his head leaning on his elbow. "Puts a crimp in the plan."

"We could throw the plan out the window? Move. Raise snow bunnies?"

Dusty told me the first time I visited he wanted this house to be somewhere he didn't have to leave if he didn't want to. And from the moment we started coming here as a family of three, it's become the place I've wanted to bring our children home to. This weekend has proven there is room for everyone here.

Dusty rolls on top of me.

"What are you doing?" I squirm.

"Catching up." His lips trail my neck and chest. "You're one stop ahead, Cees. And if you're on board, then so am I."

Thank you for reading Sliver of Truth! I hope you loved the angst in Dusty and Cece's love story as much as I loved delving in to writing such raw emotions.

Caught up in Trig and Kimber's love story? Enjoy a second glimpse into their life in the following preview of the next Shattered Hearts of Carolina book, **Holding Onto Hope…**

HOLDING ONTO HOPE

Kimber

"But are you living your best life?" I pose the question to Cece that's been on my mind as of late.

It's mill girls' day. A bunch of us are meeting up at our favorite boutique in downtown Brighton and getting coffee next door at Baked Beans afterward. Only

Sloan, Cece, and I have shown up so far. The two of them have already sifted through half of Paisley's racks while Sloan plays the role of Cece's personal stylist, something she's well-suited to.

The sun is shining through the plate glass. As glad as I am to be hanging out with my best friends this morning, my eyes haven't adjusted to the light. Thank goodness no one cares I haven't taken off my dark sunglasses. I'm using my late shift at Sweet Caroline's and the drive back-and-forth to drop my son off with his pseudo grandparents for all it's worth. But, in my defense, I didn't roll my eyes when I asked Cece if she was happy.

I love Cees and her ambition to go after a career she was meant for. But she's been so focused she's forgotten to have fun. Cece is more than ten years younger than I am, and I don't want her to have the same regrets I do about the lost years before I met my husband, Trig. I wish I'd appreciated how easy life was when I had the chance, instead of stumbling over the roadblocks I'd put in my way.

With age, I've also come to know Cece won't understand my perspective for another decade. So, a bit of playful teasing that she has to dump the tub of vanilla ice cream she's currently in a serious relationship with is as far as I'm willing to push it.

Cece shrugs with a half-hearted and self-conscious smile as Sloan, my partner in crime, continues snagging clothes off the rack and putting them up to admire the colors against Cece's flawless skin.

It's a little unfair. I've got a stupid zit on my chin—the kind that's so far under the skin it hurts like a bitch—and a ton of concealer on to hide the redness. Aren't you supposed to outgrow acne?

Stupid hormones.

The store bell jangles. Holly, the assistant manager at Sweet Caroline's, makes a whirlwind entrance, allowing

Cece to save face. Cece excuses herself before walking to the dressing room. I use it as an excuse to haul my behind back to the chaise and plant my lazy ass on its cozy cushions.

My to-go mug is resting on a side table and I take a sip, forgetting that it's decaffeinated swill. *Yuck.*

"What time did the boys hit the links?" Holly inquires.

"Too early, but it was intentional. Trig and I have plans later this afternoon and Jake is all about the nineteenth hole."

"Jake is all about any hole he can stick his putter into," Sloan mutters.

The three of us snort in unison.

"I don't care if we live in North Carolina, sane humans do not golf in January!" Cece pipes up from inside the dressing room stall.

I open a bleary eye and spy Holly twirling a countertop display.

"Will you bring me a pair of those silver dangle drop sets to see?"

"Sure thing." She hands me a card from the rack.

I brush my thumb over the intricate earrings and lift the tag, surprised it's got a slash with a markdown price.

"Gonna get it?"

"I think so." I sit and pull a bill from my wallet.

Paisley, the boutique owner and its namesake, scans and bags my purchase. I wave her off over the receipt and coins. We shop here often and I'm currently using her store sofa as a bed. So give a penny, take a penny, right? Or a buck ninety-five. It all comes out in the wash. At Baked Beans, I tip Aidy when she makes my coffee, and she lives in my attic.

I walk back to the chaise and flop down like a moody teenager, staring at the ceiling while the other mill girls finish their shopping.

In the end, Cece has an armful of clothes to wear for her new job as a pediatric physician's assistant.

"You're not getting anything?" she asks.

I hold the tiny bag containing my earrings up by my index finger.

Holly's now futzing over a display of lotions. She twists the lid on a bottle and sniffs. "This smells pretty. And familiar. Hey, Cece, do you wear this?" Her nose wiggles, taking a second whiff.

Celine sidles over. They stand around, inhaling each fruity, floral scent while Sloan is busy at the register.

I haven't had breakfast and my stomach rolls at the words, basil, watermelon, mint, and even strawberry. I'm moving past hungry to the point where my maudlin mood will be apparent if I don't start participating in the fun my girlfriends are having.

"What did you find?" I rise from the recliner and push my sunglasses over my brow, making them into a headband, but lean away from the icky perfumes. "Are we going to see Aidy?"

"Did your espresso kick in, dearest?" Holly counters the two swift questions with a pat on the arm.

"Yes, finally." I lie.

"How long until your next dose?"

Eight to ten hours, but who's counting? No one here. This hurts too much to share with my girlfriends.

"You're awful." I quip instead.

"Oh, I'm awful? Come here, let me hug you! Have you ever worked with *you* when you are caffeine-free? I'm terrorized by the idea of Owen becoming a big brother. Nine months of you drinking decaf at midnight and I'm jumping up and down when Jake drags his sorry ass into the club."

Holly's the first to pull out of the embrace, unaware my back has stiffened.

"Say what you mean, why don't you?" I stroke my long red hair back behind my shoulders.

We both snicker. I'm secure in the rapport we keep. But if Holly only knew.

"You know I will. I love you so much, I'll even buy your next grande."

There's only one thing I want more than a Baked Beans grande. Yet, I'm over holding onto hope that this month will end any differently than the others have since my son was born. I'm sick and tired of feeling sick and tired for no damned good reason.

Sloan calls me over and I slide the sunglasses over my eyes again so none of them bear witness to the tears pricking behind my eyes.

Ready to read more?
Holding Onto Hope is available now!
www.jodykaye.com/holdingontohope

Some characters are easy to write. Despite the research I did on how to incorporate stuttering into readable flowing dialogue, turning Dusty into a whole person wasn't as difficult as my second guessing made it seem when I'd first decided to write a hero with a disability.

I love how he accepts who he was, who he is, and what's important in life. He had the chance to achieve his own dreams before his accident and wants the same satisfaction for Celine.

Cece? She's another story. If you haven't realized it yet, many of the themes in Shattered Hearts of Carolina exist to make you explore the way you react.—And me… I'm totally including me in that statement.—Even in the silence of our minds, people don't like being faced with their own preconceived notions (Again, I spent a lot of my time over the winter and in the early spring sifting through my bias because the last books I've penned have dealt with heavy topics!) It's hard to admit there are times we wonder what others think of us. It was difficult to make Cece's misgivings realistic without planting a seed that a human reaction made her unlikeable. Believe it or not, writers don't ever want readers to disengage with a character because of their flaws. Many times if I don't like a heroine it's not based on their actions or inactions, but rather not liking the idea I might have made similar choices given the circumstances. Reality sucks. It's why we look to books as an escape, right? But I've also learned that storylines that don't shy away from hard topics are a hallmark of modern romance novels.

A "writing rule" to remember I've had posted in my

office for years is *characters struggle with who others think they are.* I had to skew this a bit and make part of Cece's struggle be *what will I think of myself if I can't defend someone else I claim to care for.* While Cece protected Morgan from tid-bits of their family history, she'd been protecting her heart too. She didn't need a hero to save her as much understand she'd become someone with the power to help the people she cared about.

I've had a lot of questions about the hints I've dropped about what goes on at the mill and how many books will be in this series. The latter is easy. I started 2020 with plots for eight and am working on books four and five. It may not be until six when the scope of what the guys have gotten their hands dirty with unfolds, but I hope you have better insight surrounding Carver's nature now.

This is the part where I'm supposed to thank people. I've always circled back to friends, Quinters, writing peers—like Suzanne Winslow (who was awesome enough to answer my odd questions when I ran into a stumbling block)—and MJA. But this time I need to acknowledge my sons.

Like so many kids, 2020 hasn't been easy on them. They lost out on huge milestones, which should have been celebrated with pomp and circumstance. We've become insular with virtual learning and the dynamic of our family changed with one leaving the nest. I've had to reengage and re-become the parent I was for them when they were little, tugging at my knees, and in need of my full attention. They've had to understand the balance of mom's job, and make sure I don't take myself too seriously by joking about all the half-naked men in my stock photo light boxes. (Want to actively reflect while doing your best to raise respectful feminist? Take a close look at the other side of the coin and how you'd feel if they had bikini-clad women on their laptop screens.) However, my biggest "thank you" is this: I understand for the last 5 years, mom's unconventional and embarrassing job has opened *you* up to criticism during a point in life when all kids struggle with who they are and worry about how others view them. And during a time in history when it seems as if everyone is focused on nit-picking shit they have no true interest in ever understanding, it makes everyone knowing your mom is a romance writer more difficult. I appreciate the support you give, the enormous hearts you have, and the men you are becoming. I will never have bigger fans than you, and I'll be the greatest fan of your lives.

Add your voice and help readers discover
this love story by writing a review!

Also by Jody Kaye

Shattered Hearts of Carolina
Splinter of Hope
Shred of Decency
Sliver of Truth
Holding Onto Hope
Home Wrecker
Deep Gap
Bleeding Heart
Shattered Soul

The Kingsbrier Legacy
Love Thy Neighbor
Gray Sin
Going Down

The Kingsbrier Quintuplets
Eric
Brier
Daveigh
Miss Cavanaugh
Cavanaugh
Adam
Colette
Colton

The Canvas Duet
Canvas
Imprint

To view more great titles, sign up for Jody Kaye's newsletter, or find her on social media go to www.jodykaye.com or

Scan Now!

About the Author

Jody's husband asked what she'd been doing all day. After five years she finally confessed, "When no one is around, I write."

Okay, it was more like a bunch of stammering and trying to get out of saying a thing. Jody's a writer. You want it pretty. Let's compromise.

"Just finish one," he said, challenging her to complete a story and share it. Little did he know that those words of encouragement meant they'd return from a family vacation with a wild and defiant set of quintuplets stumbling their way into adulthood. Wasn't raising their three sons enough?

A native of nowhere, Jody settled in New England for 17 years before agreeing to uproot her brood of boys and move to North Carolina. She's a part-time graphic designer and marketeer with over twenty years' experience, and full-time writer. If Jody ever gets lost, you'll find her reading, all the while hoping that her ravenous children haven't eaten all the ingredients before she's cooked dinner.